ONE MORE TOUCH

ONE FOR ALL
BOOK 2

MAYA JEAN

Alpha read by JJ and Hannah

Beta read by Lexi and Donatella

Sensitivity read by Abigail

Edited by Jennifer Griffen

Proofread by Judy's Proofreading

Cover by Books N Moods

ISBN: 979-8-9906061-6-6

 Formatted with Vellum

For JJ,
who gave me the safe space to let Mason come to life.

PLAYLIST

- Fear by Sleeping at Last
- Sires by Fleurie
- Deep End by Ruelle
- Seven Devils by Florence + The Machine
- Start a War by Klergy
- Blue Blood by LAUREL
- Mr. Sandman by SYML
- Cherry by LAna Del Rey
- You Belong to Me by Cat Pierce
- Run Baby run by The Rigs
- Find You by Ruelle
- I Found by Amber Run
- I Don't Wanna Be Okay Without You by Charlie Burg
- To Hold on to You by Luca Fogale
- Angel Baby by Troye Sivan
- Without You by Ursine Vulpine
- Two Men in Love by The Irrepressibles
- Slip Away by UNSECRET

- Daylight by Taylor Swift
- Lonely Day by Amira Elfeky
- Pull Me Down by Mikky Ekko
- Villain's Aren't Born (They're Made) by PEGGY
- Body by SYML
- Wide Eyed by Billy Lockett
- Rescue my Heart by Liz Longley
- Hurricane by Tommee Profitt
- In The Shadows by Amy Stroup
- In the Air Tonight by Natalie Taylor
- Sleep to Dream by Fiona Apple
- Where's My Love by SYML
- Like Real People Do by Hozier
- Grace by IDLES
- Adore by Amy Shark
- Free Animal by Foreign Air
- Broken by lovelytheband
- I Must Be in Love by Aaron Taos
- Drop Me Off in the Sky by Luke Wild
- Like in the Movies by Vlad Holiday
- Out of my Mind by Reuben and the Dark
- Neptune by Sleeping at Last
- Feel Something by Jaymes Young
- Wanted Dead or Alive by Empara Mi
- Hummingbird by Run River North
- Shell Suite by Chad Valley
- The War by SYML
- Like No One Could by flora cash
- Twenty Something by Nightly
- All Of The Girls You Loved Before by Taylor Swift

Spotify Playlist

DEAR READER,

Hi! It's me again. The author who's so full of anxiety sometimes I don't know if publishing is even worth it for me. But I've never been good at quitting.

The last time I did one of these was with Benji and Nolan. So I think that says a lot. Writing any sort of representation is like walking through a minefield. Why do I do it when most people find fault with it? I can't give you that answer. I put pieces of myself into every character I write, but some of them get more "me" than others. Aiden had my childhood. Nolan had my depression. Trevor had my martyrdom. Harper had my sarcasm. Reid had my sass. And now Mason has my OCD and contamination fears.

OCD is one of those things that might be hard to understand if you don't have it. I painted Mason with the brushstrokes of my OCD and gave him my hopes for where my life can go if I work hard enough. I hope even if you don't understand him, you at least understand what I've tried to do. We meet Mason partially through his OCD journey, so he's in therapy, and has medicine to help him.

Three nose taps and a smile.
MJ

CONTENT AND TRIGGER WARNINGS

- Murder and blood
- Gun violence
- Mentions of sex trafficking and bad guys being sexual predators to underage women
- Obsessive compulsive disorder that severely limits a characters life
- Anxiety spiral due to being triggered
- Obsessive cleaning
- Spiraling thoughts
- Fear of germs and being touched (contamination fear)
- Childhood cancer and mentions of past treatments and hospitalizations
- Arrest and injury of a major character
- Mentions of past parental death

PROLOGUE
PARKER

Freshman Year

"Can I sit here?" a short brunette girl asks, then bites her lower lip.

I look curiously at the empty desk next to me in the lecture hall, wondering why she'd even bother asking. "Uh, sure."

She smiles sweetly and takes the seat without a word. I count to ten slowly, then adjust my glasses until they stop sliding down my nose. I really need a new pair, but money is tight for my twin brother and me. We subsist solely on the miraculous scholarship we somehow finagled out of Eastport University.

"Hey," the girl whispers during the best part of the lecture.

I send her a severe look, hoping to silence her. "Yes?"

"I like your glasses."

"Okay."

She taps her pen on her notepad with an easy smile. "Are you free?"

I stare blankly at her. "For what?"

She stares back. "Like, for coffee?"

She is the third girl to ask this of me since I started at Eastport University. Do they want to copy my homework? I ignore her question and return to listening to the professor. I went my entire life without getting any attention, but suddenly college has brought up new opportunities. I don't care much for dating or hooking up, though I have to admit the attention is very flattering. It's nothing compared to the attention Jacob has always received. Fraternal twins are a trip. I'm convinced he sucked up more nutrients in utero to give himself an unfair edge.

When I push through my dorm room later that beautiful September day, I don't expect to see Jacob, looking exhausted, sitting on the bed with an open envelope cradled in his hands. He lifts his wary gaze to me, and a shiver rolls through me at the weight of it.

"What's that? Is it about the life insurance payout?"

We got a small life insurance payout when our mom died a few years ago, but we didn't gain access to it until we turned eighteen. Why a nurse had no will is beyond me. But between the insurance and the scholarship, I still don't know why Jacob feels the need to work.

Jacob shakes his head tiredly. "No... it's an invite to an exclusive club."

I hold my hand out for the invite, lifting it up to read it over carefully. It's for a date and time at the end of September, and there's also two checks—four thousand dollars for both of us—tucked neatly in the envelope. My eyebrows lift into my hairline at the numbers on the checks.

"Seems like free money," I say as I hand him back the envelope.

Jacob scowls. "Don't be flippant. There's no way we can go. Right?"

Well. I'm apt to say yes because it's money, and it seems sort of harmless. The address is for the other side of Eastport in the evening, so the worst part will be that Jacob will have to miss a shift at the diner.

"I think we should go."

Jacob groans and tosses himself back on the too tiny twin bed, his feet dangling precariously over the edge. "I shouldn't have said anything."

"Well, we don't lie to each other either. We're going."

Jacob winces. "Well... technically this is the second letter."

I narrow my eyes, pushing my glasses up my nose. "Explain."

"We got one a week or so ago, but I ignored it. Also, the checks were only for two thousand each then."

"What the fuck, dude?"

Jacob looks appropriately scolded. "It just felt fake."

"Okay, well, we're going now. Thanks for hiding it so we got a pay increase, I guess."

I toss my bag onto my bed, grab my shower caddy, and take the hottest shower of all existence in the communal showers. When I return, Jacob has taken his own shower and is lying on the bed with his hair damp and his fingers loosely tangled over his abdomen.

"Chin up, bro, free money," I tell him.

But Jacob doesn't reply, which has become par for the course lately. I don't know what's wrong with him, and I'm not used to seeing him so sullen. Jacob is usually the life of the party, the one everyone wants, and I've spent much of my life pretending to be as much like him as I can, despite wanting to be the opposite. I want to be at home curled up with a book, glasses on, and a mug of tea in my hand. But that's not the *cool* guy kind of evening to have it seems. Jacob's the cool one. He always has been, with his effortless looks and easygoing personality. The one everyone wanted in high school, the star athlete, and I was the twin who just barely held up to him.

"I guess we're going," Jacob says as we both cuddle into our beds for the night.

"We're definitely going." And that's that.

———

Jacob swears in irritation while hopping over a puddle in the dark. The address is a warehouse on the outskirts of the city, and the sky has a thin layer of clouds covering the stars. We both dressed in casual clothes as if prepared for a fight. We're both trained in martial arts, so at least if something crazy goes down, we can defend ourselves.

The warehouse is empty but for a laptop and briefcase resting on a chair in the center of the room. Looking down at my watch, I realize we're a few minutes early, and maybe everyone else has decided to be on time or, more likely, late to sus out if we've been invited here to be hacked apart and sold for pieces on the black market.

"At least we're first," I say brightly.

Jacob hums absently as his gaze sweeps across the room, probably carefully noting all the various exits around us. A few moments later, the sound of someone else opening the door has us both spinning around. A blond man who's the perfect copy of a Greek god walks through the doors. He's about our age, just a little shorter than us, with perfectly styled naturally blond hair, and the way he carries himself tells me he's probably the one in charge of this entire thing.

"Sup?" Jacob calls out.

The man waves as he approaches. "You got the invite too?"

"Yeah, you're not in charge?" I ask, leveling him with a suspicious look.

He rears back in surprise. "Why would you think I'm in charge? I got the invite too, just like you. I'm Hayden."

The three of us shake hands like very mature adults. We make idle chitchat awkwardly, but I zone out a little bit, more focused on the computer with the screen saver in the center of the room. The door opens again to reveal a tall young guy with light brown skin, dark, slightly wavy hair, and a permanent-looking scowl.

"So, we fighting?" the new guy calls out.

Hayden frowns at him. "Why do you think we're fighting?"

"I mean, why else would I be here with two thousand dollars deposited in my bank account?" he asks, but all I can think about is how he got shortchanged because Jacob and I each got four thousand dollars.

He finishes crossing the warehouse and comes to a stop in front of us, surveying the room, his curious gaze landing on the computer just like mine had. Suddenly, the screen saver flashes in the dark, a countdown appearing on the screen. My heart starts to race a little from the fear of the unknown, but also from excitement that maybe I'll finally get to do something other than go to school and wait for Jacob to reappear in the dorm.

The new guy glances down at his watch, then glances back up, catching my gaze.

"I'm Parker." I hold my hand out for him to shake. I wince from the strength of his grip and fight the urge to pull away. "Nice handshake."

"Ditto," he says. "I'm Dante."

"What's your degree?"

"Engineering," Dante says. "You?"

"English lit," I answer, then point at my brother. "That's Jacob, his degree is in biomedical engineering. Blond god over here is majoring in math."

"Math?" Dante asks curiously.

"I like numbers," Hayden says with a lazy shrug. "I'm Hayden."

Dante hums and crosses his arms over his broad chest. The countdown hits nine and Hayden gasps in what sounds a little like surprise from beside Jacob, but all my attention gets diverted to the computer. No person comes up on the screen, just an audio application that shows the decibels of the person speaking.

"Thank you for being good boys and showing up," the computerized voice says. "I've chosen all of you because you have a skill set I can use, and those skills are for me to know only. I'd like to start a team that gives the bad people what they deserve."

"Like Robin Hood?" I ask curiously.

The message just keeps going without any pause for my question. Great. Even a computer ignores me.

"Four missions a month, maybe more. A house will be provided for you to live in that's more secure than any other

6

house in Eastport. A stipend for school. If you want to kill a bad guy, it'll be cleaned up, and you won't be caught."

A house to live in... a stipend for school. That means no more extra job for Jacob.

"All right, well, this was fun," Dante says while making a show of clapping his hands. "Story time and two thousand dollars. Any of you want to spar with me so this night isn't a total waste?"

The three of us stare at him in confusion because it seems we're all actually considering it. Jacob roughly grabs me and tugs me over to the other side of the room.

"I don't think we should do this, it sounds too criminal," Jacob says out of the corner of his mouth.

"You can't be fucking serious," I whisper furiously.

"You seriously want to be like little miniature John Wicks?"

"Yeah! Kind of!"

Jacob rears back. "Really?"

"Well! It's better than what we're doing now and sometimes it's not enough. I want to do more. Maybe we can get back at some people and feel better about life in general."

"You don't feel good about life?" Jacob asks quietly, sounding a little afraid.

Now is not the time for this discussion. "Jacob, our mom is dead and we're just fucking going through life like a couple of aimless kids. Yeah, maybe this will give us purpose. And also the money would be nice because I don't know how long the life insurance money will sustain us. Mom would want us to be taken care of."

Jacob basically growls. "Low blow, bro."

I shrug, uncaring. "I'm doing this with or without you."

"Fuck."

"Also," I say, squinting his way, then squinting back at the other two who are standing awkwardly beside the computer. "No hooking up with either of them."

Jacob groans in agony. "The blond though!"

"No."

"Fine."

I grin, happy to have gotten my way, which is actually pretty easy for me to do with Jacob because he's a giant pushover for someone he loves. We end our side talk and return to the others. I feel pleased, but Jacob looks a little put out, which is funny because he'll probably end up enjoying this more than any of us. Give Jacob something to succeed at and suddenly he'll be the best.

Jacob squats down to grab the briefcase from under the laptop. A small sticky note that has all four of our names written on it is stuck to the briefcase. He clicks open the sides and reaches inside, pulling out four manila folders that he slowly hands to each of us, then lowers the briefcase to the ground.

I hold my manila folder in my hands like it might bite me, sneaking glances at the rest of the guys. Jacob stares down at the papers in his hands like he's been handed the codes to the nukes, but when I lean over to sneak a glance, he quickly snatches them away and mouths *later*. Okay. Ignoring him for now, I tentatively open my folder.

Inside is the lease to a house near campus that's ours scot-free. There's also some information about a monthly stipend for a couple grand a month, the keys to a Mercedes, and a specific note about me undergoing training for rifle use. Does everyone else have the same notes? By Jacob's face I'd assume not because there's nothing particularly special about mine, until I flip to the last page. There's a note about me going on separate missions from everyone else, after we're trained and have been on a handful of missions together. That seems... different.

"I got keys for a Mercedes?" I say in wonder, lifting the keys up for everyone to see. "Anyone else get a car?"

Hayden shakes his head but holds up a pair of house keys. "I got keys to the house."

"Well," Jacob says blandly, gaze flitting between the rest of us. "Hi, roommates."

Suddenly, everything settles a little inside me, and I feel a little less restless. For once something cool is happening to me. Maybe I can reshape myself into someone worth attention. A little killing for good never hurt anyone. I'm going to be *so* cool.

CHAPTER 1

PARKER

Three years later

Since Reid's kidnapping, we've been taking it easier on the missions. I don't know if it's Hayden or Robin being careful, but it's worrying. Do I like committing murder? No. But we do what's necessary to protect the people who need protecting.

It's pretty easy to incapacitate someone with one simple touch. Jacob and I have been black belts since we were kids. Mom was always at work, and we were usually at the neighborhood center trying to stay out of the trouble that kids like us often got into. We didn't need to worry Mom more by getting up to no good. But I'd be lying if I said I didn't have a decent kill count. We do what we have to do in this job, and I'm particularly good at it, especially when it comes to killing without leaving a trace.

But I can't shake the feeling that something bigger than us is happening. Something *bad*. Sure, Reid might be one of us now, but that doesn't mean we should just forget that

Dante's twink boyfriend was kidnapped and tortured solely to find out who we answer to. I've had this argument with Hayden at least five times the past few weeks to no avail, so I've effectively given up.

"Why are you staring at your book like you want it to ignite in flames?" Reid asks around a mouthful of toast covered in apricot jam.

I scowl at him. "I'm concentrating."

Reid makes a disbelieving sound in the back of his throat. "Sure."

I watch in revulsion as he dunks his apricot toast into runny egg yolk and almost gag. A muffin will have to do for me today. I slap my book shut and stand, grabbing a blueberry muffin. Reid stares at me in that weird, calculating way he often does, and I lift my head high as I flee the kitchen. The pile of shoes by the front door is nice and orderly, which is becoming more commonplace now that Reid lives with us. Dante used to be the one who picked up after all of us, but these days it seems Reid helps just as much.

I shove my feet into my shoes, grab my hoodie, and prepare myself to freeze outside. Could I drive to campus? Yes. But I'd spend more time trying to find a parking spot than it would take me to walk to class.

Once I've popped my headphones in and turned on my *angry roid music*, as Jacob calls it, I step out into the freezing January air. The sun warms the air up some, but small piles of snow still crowd the steps of the brownstones that line the short walk to campus. Out of habit, I stop in front of Mason's house. Something about him intrigues me. He'd been an anxious pile of worry through Reid's entire kidnapping, but he'd not once hesitated when he'd needed to donate blood to his brother. I get it. If Jacob needed an organ, I'd give it to him without question. That's what brothers do.

Movement in the second-floor window catches my eye. Mason talks hurriedly into a cell phone, back painfully straight. His shoulders are hunched up to his ears, every muscle in his body poised for attack. I watch him argue over the phone for a minute before he gives up with a defeated-looking sigh. His fingers rub his temples as he slowly turns around to look out the window.

Being caught should make me feel embarrassed, but oddly, I don't. Instead, I lift my hand and wave at him. Mason waves back, but he looks almost confused at himself for doing it. He promptly disappears from the window, only to reappear at the front door. Somehow, even dressed in dress slacks and a button-down, Mason looks effortlessly soft. His perfectly styled auburn hair and slight smatter of freckles adds to the softness somehow. A small smile tugs at his lips at the sight of me, blooms of red on both cheeks.

"Hi," Mason says breathlessly. He dips to look around me. "Reid's not with you?"

"Sorry to disappoint, it's just me."

Mason shakes his head. "No, not disappointed. Just surprised. Would you like some coffee? I just made a pot an hour ago, so it's still hot. Unless..." Mason's eyebrows furrow as if he's embarrassed. "You're on your way to class, aren't you?"

"Yes, but I have time." I nod toward his door, silently telling him to head back inside. Mason's smile is big and breathtaking, making my stomach clench with something I don't recognize.

I slip my shoes off by the front door and follow Mason into the sweet-smelling kitchen. Without really meaning to, I go to the sink and wash my hands. After a few days in each other's pockets during Reid's and Dante's hospital stay, it was easy to pick up on Mason's fear of germs. When I finish washing my hands and glance back at Mason, he's blushing furiously and steadfastly avoiding my gaze now.

"Coffee?" he asks, gaze firmly planted on his socked feet.

"Yes, please."

Mason waves his hand at the table for me to sit down. I watch him move around the kitchen with ease, lifting up onto his tiptoes slightly to grab a black mug. His auburn hair glows when the sun hits it just right, like rubies on display.

"Cream, no sugar, right?" he asks softly, voice timid.

He remembered. "Yes, thank you."

Mason joins me at the table, black coffee for himself, and places the extra mug in front of me. There's a tremble to his fingers that I ignore for both of our sakes. The television is on in the living room, set to some channel that's angrily discussing the state of the perpetually bad economy.

Mason sips his coffee while eyeing me over the mug, a blush still high on his cheeks. "What class are you on your way to this morning?"

"I have a lecture about science fiction, and after that is gothic literature."

"Oh, you're in your last semester, right? Fun classes saved for last."

I chuckle. "I was lucky to get into the sci-fi lecture. It fills up so fast, it felt like trying to get Taylor Swift tickets."

Mason winces in sympathy. "That's the nice thing about doing your degree mostly online like I did, not much competition for classes."

"Why'd you get an online degree?"

"Needed to take care of Reid. I just graduated last year."

"What's your degree in?"

"Political science... Thought one day I'd go into politics."

"Not anymore?"

Mason shakes his head firmly, which he does quite often. At least in my presence. My phone buzzes to indicate class will be starting in fifteen minutes, breaking the moment. Shit, it's at least a ten-minute walk. I gulp down the rest of my coffee and stand quickly, sending an apologetic smile to Mason.

"Gotta get to class. Maybe... I could stop by tomorrow too? I can bring coffee?"

"Oh no," Mason rushes, furious blush returning. "I like to make my own coffee. I have different flavored beans... Do you like caramel?"

My smile actually hurts to contain. "I love caramel."

Mason's answering grin could rival Christmas morning. I back away toward the door, grinning at him, not turning around until the last moment. It's cold outside still, and I don't know why I expected it to warm up after only a few minutes inside with Mason. I end up jogging the rest of the way to class to make sure I'm there early enough to grab a seat toward the front. The jerks who are taking this course for an easy A can sit in the back, but I want to take notes and get the most out of the class. College never seemed like much of an option unless I got a million scholarships, but when Mom died, Jacob and I were pleasantly surprised she'd somehow managed a life insurance policy for both of us. Having that money, combined with the stipend from Robin, plus paid living expenses, means college isn't the noose around my neck I'd once thought it would be.

Going on for my master's might be a little more difficult, but I'll make do. I always do.

———

Jacob's waiting outside for me after class, per usual. We're fraternal twins, so it's never felt like looking in a mirror. Jacob's eyes are a softer shade of green, and he spends more time in the gym, so his shoulders are broader, muscles bigger. I'm built like a swimmer, where Jacob is built like a quarterback. But when someone looks at us, it's probably difficult to tell us apart, unless they know us. I have three moles on my abdomen, whereas Jacob has none. Also, I wasn't sure Jacob could read until the past few years, so there's that.

"I gotta go to the store on the way home," Jacob complains without any real bite. "Dante said we could figure ourselves out." Jacob puts very obnoxious air quotes around his words. I think we'd all gotten used to the status quo of Dante being the house den mom in a lot of ways, but lately Dante—or maybe it's Reid's influence—has been putting a little bit more effort into making us all grow up. It's just *easier* to let Dante do our laundry and clean the house, not because we take him for granted, but because we all know it's one of the few ways he shows his love. He might stop going to the store, but he still does everything else, even if Reid wants to put a stop to it.

"I'm going to make pork tenderloin," Jacob says.

"Fancy. With mashed potatoes?"

"No, roasted potatoes, the little fingerling ones because Hayden will eat those."

I hum in acceptance. "He's pickier than a toddler."

Jacob shrugs. "He likes starches, comfort foods."

"Are there still brownies from last night?"

"Yes," Jacob says, nose wrinkling in annoyance. "Unless Reid pilfered them all while we were in class."

"You know Dante hides food over the fridge, right?"

Jacob pauses on the sidewalk, eyes wide with rage. "*What?*"

"Yeah, same. He hides the sour cream and onion chips over the fridge."

"That bastard!" Jacob swears, fury radiating off him. I bite back a grin, because although I don't like drama myself, I do like stirring it up amongst my roommates from time to time. Jacob and I were thirteen when Mom was diagnosed with cancer. She worked as a nurse our whole lives, never made enough money, and cancer wouldn't have been a death sentence had she had the time to get the care she deserved. Maybe that made Jacob and I easy targets for Robin, who knows, but the idea of someone suffering like our mom did could keep me up at night. Actually, it does keep me up at night sometimes.

Jacob turns left instead of going straight to head home, and I follow along with him, just happy to be spending time with him. Most days we're both caught up in either our studies or a mission. He rambles on about one of his labs, and I try to follow along, but that's the main difference between the two of us. I have a brain perfectly suited for an English literature degree, whereas Jacob is perfectly suited for the biological sciences degree he's getting so he can go on to get a PhD in food sciences. Some sort of food engineer... I'm not sure I really grasp what it is he plans to do.

"Can you grab the butter that I like?" Jacob asks before we split ways to gather food quicker.

I take the shortcut down the cereal aisle to get to the dairy. I rapidly scan the rows before landing on the butter

Jacob prefers and somehow goes through at an alarming rate. Once I've grabbed said butter, I find my twin in the vegetable aisle, combing through the potatoes to make sure none of them have cracks because that will rule Hayden out from eating them. I dump the butter into the basket looped on his arm, peeking in to find a carton of ice cream that's undoubtedly for Hayden. Hmmm.

We're quiet as we finish up at the store, using the lone cashier instead of the self-checkout aisle. She seems pleased to finally have a human to help, so we make conversation as we pack everything into a brown bag ourselves.

"Hayden was hunched over his computer when I left for class this afternoon, so maybe we'll have another mission." Jacob takes a bite out of the shiny red apple he bought, then passes it to me for a bite. "Getting bored waiting."

We pass the apple back and forth until just the core is left, then Jacob tosses it into the bag so he can throw it into the composter at home.

"Hayden seems less riled up all the time with Reid around."

"They're both little shits," Jacob mumbles, voice oddly fond.

"I like Reid."

Jacob's eyebrow wings up. "Just Reid?"

Now I'm confused. "Is there someone else living with us?"

Jacob hums but stays quiet, which is his usual way of ignoring me these days. We pass by Mason's house on the way home, and I have the odd urge to invite him along for dinner. But I'm not sure he'd come anyway, considering he barely ate when holed up with us in the hotel for two days. Now that I think about it, he'd been pretty miserable, downing some sort of medicine every few hours.

Jacob disappears toward the kitchen the second the door shuts behind us. I toe my boots off by the front door, leaning against the wall for balance. A high-pitched laugh echoes from the stairs, followed by the quick pattering of feet descending down the stairs. Reid's dyed silver-and-light-blue hair is what I notice first, followed quickly by the feral look on his face. He freezes at the bottom of the stairs as we stare at one another.

"Reid," I say.

Reid swallows thickly. "Parker, good evening."

He's been walking on eggshells with me since the cigarette fuckup last year. Probably thanks to Dante. I don't want to know the inner workings of their relationship, but it's pretty obvious they have some weird control dynamic going on. If it works for them, cool, I don't really care.

Dante descends the stairs at a much slower pace, narrowed eyes trained on the back of his boyfriend's head. I must've stopped Reid from accomplishing something that would get him in trouble because he looks like he's been caught with his hand in the proverbial cookie jar while Dante looks like he's gearing up for giving a spanking. Yikes, not how I want to spend my evening.

"I'm going to go read in the living room," I announce awkwardly. "Please refrain from making... the noises you made last night. I have schoolwork."

"There were no noises," Reid whines, perpetually annoyed by our teasing.

I lift my brows at Dante but flee before I can be told otherwise. The living room is warm from the glowing fire that Dante probably started when he got home from class since Reid likes to curl up in front of it with his sketchbook. I settle down on the plush couch with my satchel. For the second time today, I feel like I can finally take a real breath.

Grabbing my book out of my bag, I settle back on the couch to finish reading so I can get ahead on the required writing for the course. Reading has always been my favorite pastime. As a kid, we didn't have much, but the library was our safe place. Jacob gravitated to the history and science section, and I'd gone right to fiction. Always. Escaping into another person's world, into their imagination, makes my world seem a little less bleak.

I pop in my earbuds and put on some rock, but I only get a few minutes of uninterrupted reading before the couch dips at my feet. Hayden blinks coyly at me and waits for me to remove my earbuds. Great. I remove them with a sigh, waiting for Hayden to say whatever he needs from me.

"Robin says for you to expect an email for a mission tonight," Hayden says with something between a feral grin and a scowl. He loathes that I get separate missions. "Do you feel like sharing what it could be about?"

"Well, how would I know if I feel like sharing since I don't know what it'll be about?"

"Parker," Hayden says glumly, shoulders slumped in defeat.

"Hayden," I echo like the undercover asshole I am.

"I don't like that you do separate missions. We aren't there to protect you."

I poke him with the tip of my sock-covered toe. "Maybe that's the point."

Hayden's gaze shifts to the kitchen, where Jacob easily moves around fixing our dinner. Sometimes Hayden gets this look in his eyes when he's looking at Jacob that makes my stomach squirm. I really try to stay out of their business, especially Jacob's love life, but something about their dynamic has changed for the worst the past few months, after being a pretty steady stream of teasing and comfort. Just when I'm about to get the courage to say something, my phone vibrates with an incoming message. Hayden simultaneously scowls and sighs before standing from the sofa and shuffling into the kitchen. He takes a seat at the table, resting his chin in his hand as he stares forlornly at my twin's broad back.

Now that I'm alone, I tug my phone out of my pocket and read over the detailed email. It's a typical solo mission for me. Dead politician but make it look like an accident. It's set for tonight, so maybe I'll get to finish my book in peace and quiet while I'm on the lookout.

I trudge upstairs to get ready. If I want to get to Middleton right after dark, I've got to leave soon. Dressed in my typical tactical gear, I skip down the stairs to beg Jacob for an early meal, but when I stride into the kitchen, there's already a plate for me at my normal seat. Reid's in the kitchen helping Jacob with dinner while Dante stares fondly at Reid's back. I dig into the meal, knowing it'll need to last me through the evening.

"Why does Parker get separate missions?" Reid asks, because he doesn't know how to not be nosy.

Jacob sighs loudly, and a bit painfully. "My brother has a skill set that the rest of us seemingly do not have."

"And what's that?" Reid questions further.

"He's the silent killer," Dante answers, eyes still on Reid. "Also, if you think I'm the insane one in the group, Parker has once again fooled someone."

I ignore their chattering and focus on finishing my meal. Sometimes it's not worth the fight. None of them *really* know what it's like to be good at killing *and* simultaneously enjoy it. I don't particularly *like* that I enjoy it. Usually, the enjoyment makes me feel shitty. Sometimes I imagine if I wasn't using my gifts for good, maybe I'd have another outlet for my desires—one that isn't killing. Or who knows, maybe I was a serial killer in another life.

Before leaving, I give Jacob the typical loving pinch on the bicep, then head out. This is also why I've got the keys to the nice SUV because Robin wants to ensure their favorite boy gets to and from all the locations without a car breaking down.

Forty-five minutes later, I park the SUV a couple of blocks down from the mark's house. The sky is dappled with clouds tonight, giving me the cover I need so the moonlight doesn't out me. I perch myself across the street in a cropping of leafless trees. The woods behind me are quiet; it's too cold for animals to be out this time of night. I'd thought I'd get to read, but it's too dark, and I'll draw attention to myself if I use a light.

Instead, I watch. The lights in the large colonial are on, downstairs and upstairs. One car in the driveway since the mark is single. No children, no wife, just an endless bank account that he stacks with money from lobbyists and illegal stock trades. A total piece of shit, per usual. I flex my fingers in the cold, my leather gloves creaking with the movement.

What is Mason doing tonight? Maybe he's cooking that soup he seems to like so much, the Italian penicillin he called it while chattering during Reid's convalescence. He'd been painstakingly careful as he'd cooked, fingers nimble as he'd chopped, the spoon held in a loose grip. Something about him had felt so familiar, yet so very strange at the same time.

Stop thinking about Mason.

The downstairs lights turn off, lights for the stairs flicker fast, and finally only the light in the bedroom remains on. Now's my time. I jog across the street, finding the back door unlocked like Robin said it would be. Idiot. The alarm is still readying to turn on, so it doesn't catch the door opening or closing. No dog either. The man lives totally alone, making him ripe for killing.

It's easy to get from downstairs to the second floor without being noticed. No pictures on the walls, nothing to show an ounce of humanity in the man who spends his life stealing from the poor, doing everything he can to punish his constituents for daring to be born.

Pausing outside the bedroom door, I take a deep, quiet breath, then kick the door open with my boot. The senator is in the middle of undressing, a dress shirt hanging off his broad shoulders as he takes off his ostentatiously expensive watch. We stare at each other for a few stilted moments before he lunges for the dresser that likely contains the pistol Robin warned me about.

I point my gun at his head, and the senator freezes, eyes wild and pissed. "You've got to be kidding me."

"It can be easy if you don't make any wrong moves. Piss me off and you die slowly, crying for your dead mommy. If you're a good boy, you'll just take the handful of pills in my pocket and go right to sleep."

He snorts. "You've got another thing coming if you think it'll go that way."

"I think it will," I say with a cruel smile. "You see, there's a folder on your computer that contains images of young girls in compromising positions, yes? Take the pills and I wipe the computer so no one knows exactly how much of a piece of shit you are. Require me to put a bullet in your head and the computer stays the way it is."

The man swallows slowly. "Who the fuck are you? What do you want?"

I nod at the bed. "Get on the bed. I'm the angel of death."

He climbs onto the bed, barefoot, pants halfway undone, eyes watching my every move. "I'll give you more money than whoever is paying you. I've got millions, I swear. Anything, just let me live."

Snorting, I roll my eyes. "If you think I'm doing this for money, then you're stupider than I thought." I pull out the prescription bottle with his name on it from my pocket and shove it at him. "Take the whole bottle."

He curiously spins the bottle around in his hand a few times. "How'd you get my prescription for Xanax?"

"I don't really think you're in the position to ask questions. Take them."

"You don't want anything from me except for me to kill myself?"

I grin down at him in the warm lighting. "All I want is you dead. Be good and do as I say, so your legacy can remain as a piece-of-shit conservative instead of a piece-of-shit child abuser."

He dumps the pills into his hand and stares down at them, then tilts his head back to swallow the fifteen pills like Tic Tacs. The room is silent as we wait, the pills slowly starting to take over. Just as his eyes are closing and he slumps on the bed, I lean over him to grin like the nutjob I really am.

"By the way, that was all total shit. I'm going to unlock your computer, open up that fucking folder, and leave it for the cops to find so that everyone can know you were a waste of space on this earth. If there's a hell, you're going."

He makes a frightened gurgle, attempting to lift his hand to grab me, but I stand back and spend the next ten minutes setting his computer up to the folder that holds enough pictures to make most people vomit. Men like him belong hung from the rafters of every warehouse in the country, depraved pieces of shit. And all of them somehow find their way to powerful positions to lord power over the weak.

The body on the bed is still, so I slink over, pressing a gloved finger to his neck to ensure he's dead. Thank god. I sneak down the stairs like a ghost, unseen and unheard, and turn the alarm on before fleeing the house. Pretty quick mission for a weekday. I take the highway back home, listening to NPR on the way to catch up on the news I missed throughout the day.

The road home leads me by Mason's, and I don't know why I'm shocked to find the light to his bedroom still on at eleven in the evening. I pull the car over to the side, spending a few moments staring up at the curtain-covered window. Is he awake? Maybe he's asleep. He seems the type to sleep with the light on. Too many ghosts in the dark.

Grabbing my phone from the cup holder, I scroll through the application for the alarm system I installed back when I was protecting him. There's a clip of him passing the front door camera to disappear up the stairs. Everything has been armed since he traipsed to his bedroom an hour ago. He's safe and sound. For some reason, knowing that little bit of information settles my soul enough I can head back home and sleep myself.

CHAPTER 2

PARKER

I'm walking along the snowy midwinter pathway with my nose in a book when I feel the prickle of being watched. The hairs on the back of my neck rise and that squirmy, hot feeling in my stomach threatens to make me vomit.

"Hey!" the person behind me shouts when they almost slam into my back.

"Sorry," I mumble, not feeling any remorse at all.

Pushing my glasses up my nose, I look around to find the object of my now pretty furious scorn. With a loud huff, I keep walking when I realize it's just Reid staring at me from his spot across the quad. Since he's quit smoking, he's taken up sucking on lollipops, and he annoyingly pops the bubble gum that remains once he's sucked all the candy away. Dante really needs to do better about regulating Reid's behavior.

"Parker," Reid says from beside me when he appears out of thin air. Perhaps he can teleport.

"Reid."

"Hey, so, Dante's birthday is next week."

I stop in the middle of the sidewalk, again almost incurring the wrath of the person walking behind me. Reid takes mercy on my stupidity and grabs my arm, tugging me toward the quad, away from the crowded sidewalk.

"I thought his birthday was in July."

Reid snorts. "That's Hayden."

"Oh."

"You guys *suck*. You'd kill for each other, but you don't know when his birthday is."

"I only know Jacob's birthday because we have the same one."

Reid's stare is so icy it rivals the snow at our feet. "I want to throw him a party."

"Good luck!" I attempt to yank out of his grasp, but for such a little twink, his grip is firm. Jesus. "Whattttt..."

"I want to have a card night at our house, just us. Cake... drinks... *no* missions."

"Talk to Hayden," I grouse, already reaching my peak annoyance.

Reid blinks his icy blue eyes rapidly at me like I'm the stupidest man on earth. Maybe I am, compared to Hayden, at least. Just when I'm about to say something else, Reid takes a slow, deep breath, closes his eyes, then reopens them to smile an awkward, stilted-looking smile my way. It's a little scary. Looks a little like Dante's smile, if I'm being honest.

"Please assist me with throwing my boyfriend a birthday party."

Well. Shit. "Okay."

"Thank you. Are you heading back to the house? I need a ride back."

I was, but usually I stop by and watch Mason's house for a little while... but I can't tell Reid that because he'll respond like a raptor who's had their favorite toy taken from them.

He'd surely eat me alive. Especially since I can't explain *why* I feel like I have to keep protecting Mason even though he's perfectly safe in their old house that's more secure than Fort Knox.

"Fine," I reply through gritted teeth.

Reid's returning smile is incandescent. Thankfully, he's quiet as we get into the SUV and as we make the brief ride home. At least he's not smoking anymore. The thick cloud of cigarette smoke that used to follow him around would set me on edge for hours. Not that it's his fault my mother started smoking at the age of twelve and died of lung cancer before she could even reach forty. *Rarely happens to someone this young*, the doctor had said with a stumped look on his face. Of course, anything to take something from Jacob and me. The universe will always ensure cruelty to us.

Reid hops out of the car without a parting word and skips up the steps, no doubt eager to search out Dante, who's lucky enough to have Tuesdays off from going to campus. The house is warm from the heater and smells like Jacob's dark chocolate zucchini bread when I step inside. After hanging my jacket up, I run my hands through my hair and make my way toward the kitchen.

Jacob grunts in acknowledgement as he continues to furiously type on his laptop, setting a world record speed surely for how fast he can type.

"Do you know when Dante's birthday is?" I ask conversationally as I walk over to the counter to make myself a cup of coffee.

"I think... in the fall? I think he's a Scorpio."

It's my turn to grunt now. I finish making my coffee, spin around, then lean my back against the counter to aim a heavy look at him. "His birthday is next week."

Jacob's eyebrows wing up. "No shit?"

"Also, what the hell do you know about star signs?"

"Candy liked them."

"Of course," I reply with a forced smile.

"She wasn't awful."

"Sure."

Jacob stares me down. "She was a nice girl."

"Yes, I'm sure Hayden would agree."

Jacob's cheeks turn ruddy at my not-so-subtle dig. That means it's time for me to leave him alone or incur his wrath, which would consist of not allowing me any dessert for a week straight. I cut a piece of the still warm zucchini bread, then bound up the stairs. Hayden's bedroom door is cracked, so I stick my head in to check on him. He's sitting at his computer desk, head in his hands, foot tapping a silent beat against the ground.

"Yo," I call out softly.

Hayden's shoulders lower a fraction before he turns to aim a glassy-eyed look my way. "Sup?"

I push into the room and kick the door closed to give us privacy. I set the savory bread on the table beside his elbow, then stalk around the room, inspecting the various posters hanging on the wall. Most of them are from science camps Hayden went to as a kid or concerts he attended with his older brother. Comfortable silence envelops us for a while, until I turn around to check that he's eating his bread. Hayden's sweet tooth will kill him one day, but Jacob's doing his best to cut the habit by adding vegetables to anything he can as if Hayden is a wayward toddler. In some ways he is after his stilted childhood and genius.

"The mission the other night went as planned," I tell him.

Hayden wrinkles his nose, licking his fingers clean as he

shoves the last piece of bread into his mouth. With chipmunk cheeks, it's easy to forget Hayden wrangles us all for Robin.

"Saw it on the news."

I grin. "Another for the record books."

Hayden hums and turns back to his computer. I watch curiously as he tugs his notepad closer, his hand making quick scratches at it. A second later, he turns around to brandish the paper at me. Taking the offending note from him, I look down at the paper in my hand with a curious tilt of my head. I recognize that name. Wait.

"Yeah, Reid's uncle."

All the air leaves me in a woosh. "You can't be serious."

"He's coming into town to visit Mason and Reid, then attend some gala downtown."

"I can't *kill* their uncle."

"Do you want to read the brief Robin sent me that warrants it?"

I swallow hard. It's always a catch-22 after I read a brief. Sometimes it gives me the motivation I need to finish the job, to make a mark hurt, but sometimes it reminds me I'm playing judge and executioner when it's not remotely my position. But there's something inside me that likes the thrill of the kill, and that fact scares me most of all. Because when I'm done with this... When I move on after college, how am I going to get this same thrill? Hunting? I don't think so. Killing animals just makes me sick. Killing humans who don't deserve to be alive? Well, that helps me sleep deeply at night, so I don't know what to tell myself anymore.

Finally, I shake my head, and Hayden grins in a way that chills me straight to the bone. It's the smile that says *I've got your number*. But he doesn't, no one does. Tomorrow night, Senator Warton will be at the Adoria Hotel in downtown

Eastport for some gala to drum up donations for his upcoming campaign. Something about this situation makes me feel off guard.

"Reid wants to throw Dante a birthday party, by the way," I say just as I'm about to leave.

Hayden tilts his head. "But his birthday is in September?"

I squeeze my eyes shut for a second and promptly flee the room. We're all *shitty* brothers. Jesus. Dante does so much for us all and we don't even know when his birthday is. Reluctantly, it makes me admit that maybe Reid is a good boyfriend. I pass by Dante's room on the way to mine and can't help but smile at the sound of Dante's low laugh, followed by Reid's irritated grumble.

Settling into the chair at my desk, I bring up as much information about the gala tomorrow night that I can. Ticketed entry only, which means I won't be killing him at the gala. Probably better since I don't want my face splashed across headlines as the accused killer of a South Carolina senator.

I lose track of time per usual, only realizing it's dinnertime when the timer on my phone goes off. Dinner is usually promptly ready at the same time every night. Probably mostly for me. I'm not in the mood for food tonight though.

Skipping dinner

JACOB

I'll save you a plate

Hayden says he'll bring it up when he's done

Thanks

JACOB

Reid wants to make sure you know he made the asparagus

Okay

JACOB

He wants to know why you aren't more excited

OMG

YAY ASPARAGUS! YUMMY! MY PEE WILL SMELL WEIRD

JACOB

He said that was too much information

I LAUGH despite myself and return to my computer to plan tomorrow's mission. I end up deciding against letting it all go down at the penthouse the senator has downtown. Do Reid and Mason ever spend time there? Reid spends every night at our house, so I can't imagine he does. I also haven't heard any rumblings of him visiting his uncle while he's in town, so who knows what their family dynamics are. Everything will take place at the hotel.

Closing my laptop, I push away from the desk to head to my closet. My entire bedroom is utilitarian. Nothing fancy. Just a bed, dresser, nightstand, desk, white down blanket, gray walls, and a walk-in closet with my own en suite bathroom. It helps my brain to keep things as plain and basic as normal. Too much color gives me migraines.

I pick out midnight-blue dress pants, a black button-up, and a harness to match. The familiar weight of my gun and tranquilizer comfort me. Although, I'm not going to kill the senator with either, they're just for my protection. The man seems to like to drink, so I'll sneak into his room, give him a bottle of liquor from the bar with the bartender's fingerprints all over it, and mix some of his blood pressure pills in so it looks like an accidental overdose. Easy as pie, as my mom used to say.

After a scalding hot shower to warm my bones, I return to the bedroom to find a plate of salmon on my desk, along with a tired-looking Hayden reclining on my bed.

"I can tell Robin no," Hayden says apropos of nothing.

"Absolutely not."

Hayden closes one eye, then the other, no doubt trying to sus out if I'm full of shit or not. Which I am totally full of shit. I *really* have a bad feeling about this one.

"I can come with you."

"No, you know the rules. Only I get my hands dirty alone."

"I still don't get why," Hayden whines.

That's for me to know and for them to never find out. Yeah, I have a particular skill set none of them have, but I also enjoy it in a way none of them ever will or could. Can I make a living as a hired hitman for real after college? English literature professor by day, hired hitman by night. I could pull it off. Maybe. I sigh as I drop my towel to tug on a pair of boxer briefs. I can feel Hayden's eyes on my back—the familiar territory of scars from fights over the years, the hastily sutured wounds that would've killed me had Mandy not been readily available for us.

"Claude is still out there, by the way," Hayden announces from where he continues to lounge on my bed, the perfect picture of a Greek god.

"I'm aware."

"You've heard nothing yet?"

I shake my head as I toss myself into the desk chair to eat my dinner. Hayden stares at me a little longer but swings himself up out of the bed to leave the room, seemingly satisfied with the answers I've given him. Once alone, I devour my dinner, then finally get back to doing the most important task at hand, my gothic fiction essay.

———

The next evening, I leave the house under the cover of darkness. A haze of low clouds blots out the stars, only giving me a view of the full moon every few minutes when a cloud passes by. I go over the evening in my head as I make the drive into town. I'll park a few blocks away and make the walk as incognito as I can. After a few minutes at the bar, I'll grab a bottle of scotch while the bartender is distracted. I'll sneak up to the senator's room through the security elevator after Hayden has made the security cameras "glitch" for a thirty-minute window. I'll poison the alcohol with his blood pressure pills, then wait in the closet to watch him drink and die. Easy peasy.

Parking downtown is always a shit show, so I roll up to the lot that valets typically use.

"Hey! I'll give you two hundred cash to let me park my car here for one hour, no questions asked," I ask once I've rolled the window down.

The young guy grins and holds out his hand. "Pay up."

Two hundred dollars later I'm parked in the lot and

working my way toward the hotel a few blocks over. People pass by but I ignore them. Instead, I keep my focus on the mission at hand. Clenching and unclenching my hands a few times, the leather of my gloves makes that eerie creaking noise that usually sets me on edge. The Adoria Hotel is one of the oldest and classiest hotels in the entire state. The doorman stands out front helping people still arriving for the gala, a thick red carpet underneath their feet.

The alleyway beside the hotel is so clean I could almost pretend I'm inside the hotel. No garbage stench, no piss stains. Amazing. I look up toward the security camera that's blinking red above me, waiting for the light to disappear, and once it does, I take that as a wink from Hayden that it's safe to start the mission.

It's quiet when I push inside, despite the gala being in full swing just a few floors above. The hotel bar is a couple of hallway turns inside and I keep my suit jacket on tight to hide my harness. My habit of pushing my glasses up my nose when nervous eats at me, but then I remember I'm wearing my contacts for this mission. The bar is dark, warm light from the chandeliers giving it a certain kind of ambiance. I beeline for the bar with a single-minded focus. Scotch.

The bartender is a woman only a few years older than me, yellow-blonde hair, short, with flower tattoos on her shoulders.

"Hi," I say, voice a little low, smile a little forced.

She blinks at me for a minute before grinning back and leaning against the bar. "Hi, sugar."

Yuck. "Two fingers of scotch, please. The most expensive you have."

"You sure about that?"

I wink at her. "Yes, please."

"Identification, please," she shoots back. Fuck.

I fumble for my wallet and drag out an identification with my fake name. I also toss her a fifty-dollar bill while I'm at it.

Once satisfied, she grabs the brand-new bottle of scotch behind the counter, then pockets the fifty into her bra. Normally, I'd like to pretend that it does something for me, but not tonight. Nerves have me too rattled. Another patron calls her away for a moment, so I use that as my chance to lean over the bar to grab the full bottle of expensive scotch. Perfect. I sneak away, used to hiding in corners to not be seen.

The security elevator is right where the hotel plans said it would be. I take deep, slow breaths once I get inside and hastily punch in the code Hayden guaranteed me would work. When the light turns green, I take another relieved breath. Maybe tonight will go exactly as planned. That would be great.

Reaching the penthouse floor, the doors open to reveal deep mahogany wood floors, stark white walls, and a dark red door at the end of the hall. The swipe card Hayden programmed for tonight gets me into the dark hotel suite, alerting me to the fact Senator Warton is definitely still down below at the gala. I place the scotch on the table by the door, along with the pre-typed note thanking him for some bullshit that I don't give a shit about.

His medicine is easy to find in his bathroom. Grabbing the bottle, I shake out half the pills, then return to the foyer table to work my magic. I open the scotch and drop the pills in, then hurriedly screw the top back on, grab my lighter, and light the edges to reseal it so it looks like it's never been opened. Dipping into a squat, I watch as the pills slowly dissolve in the alcohol. Five minutes later, I'm shaking the bottle to ensure they're all mixed in when I hear the card swiper ding. Fuck.

I scramble toward the hallway closet and make it inside just in time to hide myself from view. Heart pounding, sweat dotting my neck, I wait for the senator to come in and drink the scotch, but everything went a little too perfectly today, so I don't know why I expected this part to go perfectly as well. A mission always has to have a hiccup or two.

My breath catches in my lungs when Mason follows anxiously behind the senator into the room. Mason's eyebrows are furrowed, hands in tight fists at his sides. What-ever the senator is murmuring to him doesn't reach my ears, but Mason gets angrier and angrier with each lowly uttered word. Every protective instinct in my body alights again just at the mere fact Mason is alone in the room with the senator, someone vile enough I've been deemed fit to kill him.

"I told you, this is the way it's going to be, kid."

"But I've done enough. There has to be a point it ends," Mason argues, a plea in his shaky voice.

The senator finds the scotch, tips it back with a slightly cruel smile, and proceeds to twist it open and pour himself a glass. Oh fuck. He's going to drink it right now and drop dead in front of Mason. Then I'll never get out of here. I swipe a hand across my forehead and close my eyes tight. *Think of something, Parker. Think of a way out of here.* The booming sound of a gunshot shakes me out of my thoughts, and I open my eyes to the sight of Mason standing over a gasping sena-tor. The gun hangs loosely from Mason's fingers, a dazed, scared look on his face like he can't believe what he's just done.

Double fuck.

CHAPTER 3

MASON

Two days earlier

I 'm going to buy a gun.

Do I want to buy a gun? No. But I think I need to be prepared to take serious action against my uncle when I see him in a few days. Will I kill him? The likelihood of me killing someone is small, but one must always be prepared, especially when one's uncle is asking you to bring your gay brother to events as a dog and pony show to prove said uncle is not a veritable awful person. I will not allow Reid to be the token family gay. Never mind that I myself am also gay, but that's easy for Uncle Marc to ignore when I don't date anyone because I'm allergic to touch and scared someone will give me a yet-to-be-discovered disease that makes my childhood cancer come back and kill me.

My brain is not a friendly place.

But I am buying a gun.

I tug the ball cap on my head down lower as I skulk across the sidewalk toward the gun shop. The sun is bright as ever today, but the air is beyond chilly, and I shiver as I work my way closer to the gun shop that emanates bad vibes. Guns are *bad*. I *hate* guns. I hate the idea of using one even more. But needs must.

The gun shop smells like oil and metal. My skin feels too small and my throat feels tight as I bury my hands in my pockets to look around. Thankfully, no salesperson beelines it for me, probably because of my ball cap and general *don't approach me* attitude.

All the research I did said a simple handgun will suffice.

I wish I could ask Reid or his boyfriend, Dante, or even handsome-as-hell Parker, but asking for advice for this would also mean explaining to them how I've been hacking for my uncle for the past few years and think he's a very bad man. I do not want to explain any of this, nor do I want to open up questions about myself. So.

"Can I help you?" a guy in his mid-thirties asks from behind the counter.

I point at a black metal gun. "I want that one."

"There's a two-day waiting period," the man patiently explains.

I do the math in my head real quick. If I buy it now, I'll have it the morning of the gala. That's perfect. I smile the best I can. "That's perfect. I mean... I can wait."

The man smiles benignly. "Can I see your ID for this purchase? It's eight hundred dollars, not counting any ammunition."

"Eight hundred dollars," I mutter under my breath while digging for my wallet. I hate this part. The guy is going to touch my ID, but at least it's the fake ID and cash so that I don't have to disinfect my entire wallet when I get home.

Thankfully, the guy is quiet through most of the transaction and the required paperwork. Once I take my pretend driver's license back from him, my fingers tremble as I collect the documentation that'll let me pick up the gun in forty-eight hours. The air outside is a welcome slap to my face, lessening the anxiety that threatens to overtake me.

Tugging my ball cap back down, I hurriedly walk the twelve blocks home. I would rather die than get into a rideshare, plus it's not like I want someone knowing I was at the gun store. Oh my god, the gun store. I'm losing my marbles.

Once I get back home, I strip myself down, toss my clothes into the washer with my disinfectant detergent, and climb into the shower to scrub myself down. My body is pink by the time I'm done. Shit. I forgot to disinfect my wallet and everything inside it. I don't feel like doing it right now, but it'll bother me if I don't, turning into a spiral of thoughts that will make it impossible to sleep until I do it. Even with my medicine to control my obsessive-compulsive disorder, I can't escape the need for everything to be clean in my house. No germs in sight, ever.

After tugging on exercise shorts and a baggy T-shirt, I stomp down the stairs to get to work disinfecting my wallet. And once that's done, I can finally relax for the rest of the day. What that means is I'm going to cook my mother's pastina recipe and watch *The Goonies* for the millionth time.

Cooking pastina always reminds me of my mother. When I had cancer, she cooked the pastina so often that Reid got sick of it. Only his rebellion made her cook something else; even then, it seemed to be under duress. Thinking of younger Reid makes me feel sad and lonely, especially now that he's moved in with Dante. It's nice to not have anyone in my space for once, but despite the anxiety Reid caused me, it was comforting to not live alone in this house that's too big for one person.

I'm lonely, is what I am.

And I'm thinking of killing my uncle in two days because he is an awful bully who demands more and more of me each time we speak. Dig up dirt on this person, that person, now this senator, now that congressman. One day his dirty deeds are going to get me tossed in jail, which is a death sentence for someone with germ fears like my own.

I finish cooking the pastina and settle onto the couch to watch *The Goonies*. I stare for a moment at the empty spot on the sofa where Reid always sat with his sketchbook, wishing maybe I could call him, ask him how his day was, just tell him I love him. But knowing Reid, that would only irritate him, and I'm tired of irritating Reid. Giving him blood after his accident will have to be my love declaration for this decade.

I wish it was time for Parker to go to class so he'd stop by for a cup of tea or coffee. It's so nice when he visits. What would he think if I told him all the shit my uncle makes me do? All the evil, vile things I've researched so Marc can bury an opponent. Sometimes I wonder about digging up dirt on my uncle and threatening him with his own dirty deeds.

————

I hate wearing suits. I also hate guns. I hate galas. I hate my uncle. If I hadn't taken antianxiety medicine before stepping into the hotel, I would surely have broken out in stress hives. Itching while being anxious about itching is the worst, but also very common. And it also very frequently happens to me.

But not tonight.

The gala is in full swing, and I feel sick.

The room is loud. Everything is closing in on me as I stand against the wall. Hoping no one will notice me. Hoping maybe Marc will forget he wanted to see me alone in his room afterward. I promised myself that if he asks about Reid one more time, I'm going to kill him.

The gun burns against my back where I have it tucked into the tight band of my dress slacks. Someone laughs to my right, making the hairs at the back of my neck stand even more upright. My stomach turns when another person walks too close to me, not touching, but close enough to make me feel the vague need to be sick all over the marble floor.

I think I'm having an out-of-body experience.

My palms sweat as my uncle makes an impassioned speech to the crowd, talking about *family values* and *returning to American decency*. Oh my god, I should kill him just for that. He's such a piece of shit. How my father was related to this man is beyond me. How I'm related to him is beyond me.

I don't eat the meal provided. I don't drink any drinks. All I can do is stand here and wait as the room closes in and the hour of my decision inches closer. What am I going to do?

CHAPTER 4

MASON

Present

Life is full of moments that either go down in your memory bank to never be forgotten, or they go down as useless information to be used as dream creation fodder for your brain. Two seconds ago will, sadly, go down in the history books for my brain. I stare blankly down at my uncle as he gasps through his last breaths, real fear written across his wrinkled face. I should feel bad—after all, I just took a life —but I don't. Instead, my normal anxiety just starts to ramp up.

When that last sparkle of life disappears from his eyes... it hits me what I've done. Holy shit. I just killed my uncle, a sitting US senator. Oh my god. What have I done? I'm going to end up in prison. Reid will have no one. I'm not going to last a day in prison. There are so many germs there, so many things that'll trigger my obsessive need to clean, to *be* clean, to *not* get sick. I'm going to catch some strange disease they've never heard of, and then I'm going to get cancer again, and Reid will be left all alone in the world and—

"Mason." A voice interrupts my spiral.

Gasping for air, heart racing out of my chest, I tear my gaze from my dead uncle to find Parker standing a few steps away from me.

"Parker?" I ask, my voice distant to my own ears.

Parker holds his hands out like he's soothing a lion reared for attack. "Hey, Mason. What are you doing here?"

"I... I..." I take a deep breath and flex my fingers, letting the gun drop from my hand to the floor. Parker swoops in to catch it at the last second in his gloved hands.

"Let's just put this away," Parker says matter-of-factly. He turns the safety on, then carefully tucks the gun into an empty slot on his holster. It fits perfectly. "So. That gunshot was pretty loud, and there's going to be a lot of people coming up here soon. How would you feel about taking a ride with me?"

"Where?" I ask, tongue thick in my mouth.

Parker smiles, soothing me. "Anywhere you want to go. Come with me?"

Parker holds out his arm, not his hand, and gives me the choice to latch on. Somehow my fear of germs, fear of death, is a distant thing after just killing Uncle Marc. Fuckkkkk. My heart rate starts to lift again when I move to glance down at him, but Parker dips so that he stays in the way of my frightened gaze. He smiles again, calmly, wisps of hair escaping the band at the back of his head. His hair is long now. I don't remember it being that long. Is it soft to touch? God, I wish I could touch someone.

"Where are your glasses?" I ask dumbly.

Parker smiles again. "I wear contacts during missions."

"Oh." That makes sense.

"Mason, we need to leave. I don't want to touch you, I know you don't like that, but we've got to go."

"Okay," I agree without knowing what else to do.

Parker's smile doesn't change, even as he shimmies his arm a little to invite me to touch. Time slows down. I grip his muscled bicep, feeling it flex under my fingers as he leads us out of the quickly shrinking hotel room.

"Hey, I need you to cover us out of here, no blind spots. Yeah, *us*. I'll explain when I get home. Make sure everyone's awake," Parker whispers while carefully guiding me into the elevator. He smiles at me again and my heart rate slows, less frightened rabbit and more worried teenager before an important exam.

I keep my eyes on Parker as he navigates us out of the hotel without being seen. It's some sort of miracle that he was there. What are the odds? Actually... Wait, what *are* the odds? When we're safely out of the hotel, under the dark of night and ensconced in the G-Wagon, it hits me.

"Hey, so I know I just killed my uncle, but why were you there?"

"Oh," Parker says on a laugh. "I was supposed to kill him tonight."

Oh. *Oh.* "Sorry for ruining your plans?"

"Yeah, well..." Parker flicks his hand. He reaches forward to change the Spotify playlist on the car to something with far too much electric guitar for my taste. "So uh... is that the first time you've..."

"Killed someone?" I ask, voice higher pitched than usual.

Parker grimaces and nods. "Yeah."

I squeeze my eyes tight to make the sight of Uncle Marc dead on the ground disappear. There are just some things one can never unsee. Parker's phone rings, and I open my eyes to see Dante's number appear on the screen in the car. Parker hits Dismiss and returns his hand to the steering wheel, tightly gripping it.

I try not to sneak glances at him, to look out the window, but it's hard when he's saved me for the *second* time. Although, he probably wouldn't tell the story the same way regarding the first time he'd saved me. But Parker had tried to get the men to leave me alone last time, fighting against them so they'd stop touching me once I'd been triggered. He'd distracted them enough to make them abandon me, earning himself a concussion in the process, and the attackers fled to no doubt assist in Reid's day-long torture.

Maybe I have a bit of a hero complex for Parker, combined with the tried-and-true gay-boy crush on the hot straight boy. I can't help it. Parker ticks every box I have. He's well-read, handsome, competent, and, as far as I can tell, he's a patient, kind sort of man. So basically he's my wet dream come to life. But it doesn't matter because he's

A.) straight

and

B.) I can't have sex because I'm afraid someone will infect me with a strange disease that'll kill me.

I love having OCD and the anxiety that goes hand in hand with it. Life is a *joy*.

"So, we're going to have to tell the boys," Parker informs me when we pull off the highway.

My heart starts to race again just at the thought of telling Reid what I've done. What I'm going to have to explain. So many years of... Fuck. I don't even know how to attempt to explain everything. Also, what if Reid hates me for killing

Uncle Marc? Rationally, I don't think he will, but it's still a worry. All I ever do is worry.

"Can't we just say you killed him?" I ask with an awkward grimace.

Parker grunts and swings his head toward me. His dark green eyes are squinted, the corners a little wrinkled, and another piece of his dark brown hair has fallen out of the tiny bun at the back of his head. Beautiful people being near me should be illegal because of my anxiety.

"I fear that this one is going to make the news, Mace." Parker taps the steering wheel and returns his attention to the road. But the nickname makes my heart race faster than killing Uncle Marc had. Something is *deeply* wrong with me. "None of them would believe I killed a man point-blank with a gun. My methods are a little... cleaner."

"So how were you going to kill him?" I inquire while turning in my seat to face him.

Parker wrinkles his nose. "I'd poisoned the bottle of scotch that's now in the back seat of my car. The last thing we needed was them finding trace amounts of his medicine in it and realizing he was going to die tonight no matter what."

"But why were you going to kill him? Your... your boss asked you to?"

Parker squeezes the wheel tight and ignores me. The lights of downtown Eastport brighten the sky so the stars disappear, the night sky looking hazy and overcast. No snow on the ground at least, not anymore. The closer we get to the townhouse, the more I start to sweat. I seriously don't know how I'm going to explain all of this to Reid. And now the added element of Parker... God, this is such a clusterfuck. Which is how I should've assumed it would go because everything I touch turns to shit.

The car comes to an abrupt stop inside the garage, but Parker doesn't turn it off. He angles his body in the seat so that he can face me, and like there's a string connecting us, my body mirrors his before I even realize it. He reaches out as if to touch me, then retracts his arm, letting his hand come to rest on the gearshift between us.

"I'm sorry this is the way your evening is going. Now is your chance to tell me anything you don't want the boys to know. I can help you... conceal some things. Not everything, but some things."

Why is his willingness to lie for me so sexy? "I had to kill him to protect us."

Parker leans forward a little, face close enough that I can feel his breath on my face. Normally I'd be leaning back, pulling away, stepping out of the car to get air, but after the events of the evening, I don't quite feel the need to put as much space between us.

"Protect you from what?"

"Him," I whisper. "I... He wasn't a good man. That's probably why you were tasked with killing him."

"Well," Parker says with all the finality of a man walking into a lion's den. "This is the second senator to die in days, so we are up shit creek without a fucking paddle. And I'm not sure even Robin can help us clean this one up. Hopefully neither of our faces were caught on camera."

"Fuck."

"Yeah," Parker agrees succinctly. "Let's go face the music."

I follow behind Parker into the house that's much more alive than mine. The house is lived in and comfortable, and it also smells like banana bread. My stomach grumbles because I haven't eaten since this morning. I was too anxious knowing that I was going to probably, most likely, definitely kill Uncle

Marc before the end of the evening. Parker leads me to the living room, where there's a fire going and all the boys are patiently sitting on the sofa.

Reid jumps up, hands wringing in front of him, probably with the effort to not reach out to touch me. Reflexively, I reach up to tap my nose three times, our universal signal for *nothing hurts* and *I love you*. The tension bleeds from Reid's shoulders and he takes a very deep breath, then narrows his sharp gaze on Parker.

"What the hell is going on?" Reid demands, arms crossed in front of himself, foot tapping anxiously. He holds a hand out when Parker tries to speak to Hayden. "I'm asking, so talk to me."

"Fucking chihuahua," Parker mumbles under his breath. He glances at me as if considering how to handle the moment to best work for me. "I had a mission downtown at the Adora. That's where I ran into Mason."

Reid's brows furrow in confusion. "Okay? And?"

"I killed Uncle Marc," I say bluntly.

Obviously no one else understands the depth of the statement, except for Reid. His chest stills and his eyes turn confused, almost shocked. He closes his eyes tight, then reopens them as if rebooting his reality.

"Sorry, I think the matrix glitched. What did you say?"

"I killed Uncle Marc," I repeat.

"Yeah... Yeah, I got that. But why would you... I don't understand."

I feel my heart rate start to spike, sweat prickling at the back of my neck. This is so damn hard to explain. All of it. How do I explain this?

"Pause," Hayden drawls, coming to stand right behind Reid. His nose wrinkles as his gaze flicks from me to Parker. "I think we're missing some integral parts here." Hayden points at me. "You killed your uncle, awesome news." Hayden then points at Parker, eyes narrowing. "But why did you get involved? You could have just let it be."

Parker rocks back on his heels and whistles. This will be interesting for sure. All the boys continue to stare at Parker as he seemingly glues together a story that'll get us out of this.

"Your uncle was my next mark," Parker says to Reid.

"What?" Reid laughs, seemingly half in shock and half in fear. "The matrix keeps glitching. I thought you said that you were also there to kill my uncle."

"Reid..." Parker begs, a rare show of vulnerability.

Dante stands from the sofa just as Reid takes a furious step toward Parker. I instinctively take a step back, not wanting to be touched, not having the strength to withstand being touched during such an intense moment. The air grows thick with tension, everyone staring at Parker like he's the one who actually did the murdering. Nobody blinked an eye when I said I killed my uncle, but now everyone is pissed at Parker? I don't get it. Dante wraps his hand around the back of Reid's neck and squeezes, making my younger brother close his eyes in what looks very close to relief.

Dipping down to whisper against Reid's ear, Dante's words are so soft that nobody but Reid can understand them. Reid's eyes reopen a moment later after nodding in agreement to whatever Dante said. The tension ratchets down a few degrees when Reid returns to a wingback chair beside the fire, curling up so that his feet are tucked beneath him. Dante sits in front of him, arm thrown over Reid's lap like an anchor.

"Alrighty, let's start with you, Parker," Hayden says, hands on his hips, golden-blond hair messy atop his head. Every time I see him, he looks exhausted. "The mission Robin had for you tonight was to kill Senator Warton from South Carolina. Did you succeed?"

"Obviously not," Parker replies, teeth clenched.

"Cool." Hayden swings his gaze to me. "How did you end up at the Adora Hotel in the depths of downtown Middleton? And what in the world made you kill your uncle?"

"That's kind of a long story..." I avoid everyone's gaze to stare down at my shoes.

"We've got nothing but time," Dante calls out from the floor.

Clearing my throat, I'm oddly grateful when Parker moves a few inches over—not close enough to touch, but close enough I can feel the heat of him radiating toward me, a comforting balm.

"It started when I gained custody of Reid. Uncle Marc threatened me. Said that if I didn't do what he asked, he'd put this really... awful story in the tabloids about us. Make us look depraved, especially after Reid was arrested at seventeen for... Yeah." I pause and take a deep breath while rubbing my thumb and index finger together. "So I started hacking into political opponents' computers and finding dirt on them so that he could smear them. That's all it was ever supposed to be. Just harmless stuff. But then he started asking for me to get Reid to go to campaign events with him to show that he's, like, got a queer family member. To prove he's not awful. He said if I did that, he'd wipe away this information he had on Reid. He'd never share the information, but he said a lot of bad people are aware of Reid. That it was going to end up at my front door. That's exactly what he said."

"So you killed him?" Hayden presses, eyes narrowed.

"I-I was going to just threaten him." That's the truth. I

wasn't going to kill him. I *wasn't*. "But then he started talking about how he wanted me to hack into sitting US senators and members of Congress to get information on them, ones who aren't even running for reelection, and I got scared. I realized he was never going to let us fucking go. He was never going to just... fucking let me be. And I've lost so much already. I can't lose Reid too."

Reid's watery gaze pings back to me, his face hard. "You killed him because of me."

"No," I say with a firm shake of my head, because I'm not getting my point across well. As always. "I killed him so we'd finally be free."

"Well, now you might end up in prison." Hayden lifts the heel of his hand to his forehead and lets out a frustrated-sounding breath. "I'll contact Robin and see if there's anything we can do for cleanup. I know for sure you weren't caught on camera leaving, neither of you, and Parker wasn't caught coming in, but you were probably caught on camera with your uncle if you were at the event. Were you at the damn gala?"

I grimace and nod.

Jacob swears from the sofa. "Holy fuckkkkkk."

"Can't... Can't Robin fix this for us?" Parker asks, a hopeful edge to his voice.

Hayden turns his head to stare outside, then turns back to Parker. "We'll fucking see. But you already killed that senator a few days ago, so I am afraid we are in serious trouble here. People are going to be suspicious."

"Oh my god, you killed Senator Martin?" Jacob asks from the couch, eyes wide, body already half risen from the sofa.

Jacob's movement stops when Hayden lifts a hand in the universal gesture for *stop*. Why does everyone keep getting angry at Parker? He's just doing his job. I turn to stare at him, only to find he's already looking over at me, that same confused, curious look on his face from earlier. His pale skin, dark green eyes, messy overlong hair, and a small beauty mark on the elegant line of his neck has me transfixed so that I can't tear my gaze away. Such beauty contains a cost, I guess. I remind myself that although he's the most beautiful man I've ever seen, he's saved me multiple times, he's also a ruthless killer who has a body count I assume is very high.

"I'm going to step outside and make a phone call." Hayden points at Jacob when he starts to rise. "By myself. The rest of you just fucking stay out of trouble."

Hayden flees the room with a black cat hot on his heels. When Hayden steps outside, the cat I briefly met the last time I was here sits at the door forlornly, patiently waiting for their person to come back inside. Cats are nice in theory, but all the germs... I shiver to think about it.

"Scully is very clean," Reid announces from the chair, seemingly reading my mind. "She's a good girl. You should pet her."

"No... No, I don't think I can. I mean, what if—"

"All right, Mason." Reid interrupts me with a long-suffering sigh.

I fight tears at the idea of letting him down again. Squeezing my fingers over my eyes, I take a stuttering breath that hurts a little in my ribs. Maybe that's my heart. I can't tell these days. Maybe I have cancer again, or maybe I'm going to have a heart attack. Oh. That pain in my chest is definitely a heart attack. All the stress has given me a blockage and my heart is going—

"Hey," Parker says softly.

I blink rapidly and look over to find him staring at me

again, all sharp angles, mouth soft in the approximation of a smile. Oh. My mind quiets when I look at him, like one of those anchors that I find when doing my counting to prevent an anxiety attack.

"Hi," I whisper, angry at the audible shake in my voice.

"Want some tea?"

Yes. Yes, I do. Their kitchen is clean and I trust their food. I nod and feel some weird warmth blossom in my chest when Parker's smile turns genuine, turns real just because I agreed to drink some tea. He tilts his head toward the kitchen, and I follow him without a word. He tugs the chair at the island out for me, and I take a seat, grateful to just breathe because tonight feels like a runaway freight train. I watch as Parker moves comfortably around the kitchen, with the ease of a man in his own home.

He fills the kettle, then stands at the stove to wait for it to whistle. A few moments later, he fills two mugs with hot water, carefully plopping a tea bag in each mug. The warm smell of peppermint rises up, settling all my nerves. We sit in silence for a few stilted moments as the tea takes forever to steep. Parker watches me with slightly narrowed eyes as I lift the mug and take a hesitant sip. It's still too hot, but the scalding heat of the tea helps ground me in the moment.

"It's going to be all right," Parker assures me. He leans against the island with his elbows, some of his hair still escaping his messy bun.

"I killed someone. I can't go to prison."

Parker's eyes narrow and his jaw tightens. "You aren't going to prison. I won't let you."

"Why?"

"Why what?" Parker asks, confused.

"Why won't you let me go to prison? I killed a man. My

uncle, to be more exact. And to be honest, I should feel worse about that, right? I took a life. It wasn't my life to take."

I take another sip of the tea to settle my nerves that are rapidly starting to send me into anxiety-attack territory. Parker just keeps staring at me. It feels like he's looking through me—not trying to figure me out, but trying to see to the root of me. I am not sure I really like it. I don't think anyone on earth actually knows me.

"I've killed ninety-five people."

Well. That puts things into perspective. "Why?"

Parker shrugs, looking down at his tea to avoid my curious gaze. "Bad people should die."

"But why do we get to decide if someone is bad?"

"Sometimes the judge and jury don't do their jobs, and other people need to take care of the rotten pieces of society who don't belong because they find a way to escape their consequences."

I hum as I think over his argument. There are a lot of bad people in the world who just get away with everything. My uncle was one of them. He made sure kids lost their Medicaid, voted for laws that took away the rights of queer spouses to be with their partners on their deathbeds, fought against life-saving dollars going to other countries for things like ending fucking malaria—things any normal human being would be okay with, my uncle had wanted no part of. Is the world a better place without him in it? Yes. But it feels wrong that I was the one to decide he should die.

"Your uncle was going to die tonight no matter what. If you hadn't shot him, then the 400 milligrams of lisinopril that I put in his scotch would have killed him." Parker leans even farther forward, lowering his voice so I have to strain to listen. "Pretend I killed him so you don't have to live with the guilt, okay?"

"How do you live with it?" I ask, because I genuinely want to know how.

Parker taps his fingers against his temple. "Make these little boxes in your head. I envision a cardboard box, fill it with all the memories of the people I killed, then I tape it up, and store it away in this closed room in my brain."

"That's a serious coping mechanism."

Parker chuckles, and the sound rolls right through me. He has a nice laugh. It's just like his voice—deep, a little melodical, and *real*. Everything about Parker is real. Too real.

"We all have to find ways to cope with life, right?"

And that hits me like a punch to the gut, because I'm coping by making my world as small as I can. Yeah, the medicine helps, but it's not a cure-all, and my OCD will always be a part of me. At least I don't have my compulsions anymore, it's just the anxiety of... life that remains with me. The fear of getting sick. The fear of dying. But not feeling the need to wash my hands hundreds of times a day is a nice trade-off.

"Hello," Hayden says as he slides the door open to step inside. "Your uncle's body is gone."

"Huh?" Parker asks with a deep frown. "Like, Robin cleaned it up?"

Hayden shakes his head furiously. "The crew got there to disappear it and his body was gone. No blood. No body. Nothing."

Parker looks even more confused. "Uh?"

Reid joins us in the kitchen. "Wait, what?"

Hayden frowns and huffs. "Listen, I already said it. His body is gone. I don't know what else to tell you. But for now, we sit and wait." Hayden aims a steely look at me. "I think you should stay here."

"Oh no... No. I need to be in my own home."

"Then one of us will stay there with you," Hayden supplies with an absolutely fake grin.

"No... No."

"I'll stay with him," Parker says as he straightens up. "We'll stay here tonight, then tomorrow move back into his house. I'm comfortable with my alarm system still on the house. I reinforced it after last time."

Wait.

"I already have an alarm system," I say in confusion.

Parker snorts in obvious disbelief. "Sure. You purchased that out of the box from the security company, right? It's half-assed, just feels nice because it's all on your phone. Mine's better."

I blink slowly at him. "Okay."

Reid makes an aggrieved, frightened sort of sound behind me. "Why is it always something? Why can't we ever have a normal week? Just one normal week."

"Baby," Dante pleads.

Reid shoots him a glare. "No! Now we have to deal with this too. We all need a fucking vacation."

"This is a good enough time to tell everyone we're going to Arizona for spring break to visit my parents." Dante glares at Hayden when the other man tries to interrupt him. "No, we won't be working. Also, we won't have our phones with us."

Then Dante grabs Reid's arm and bodily drags him up the stairs without another word. A second later, a bedroom door slams and quiet once again envelops the kitchen. I want to say something to diffuse the tension, but I've never really been good at that. I'm more of a wallflower, although wallflower alludes to the object being pretty, something desirable, and I'm definitely not that. So maybe I'm more of a wall... wallsocketwrench.

"I'm tired, and if I don't get at least six hours of sleep, I will fail my exam tomorrow," Hayden complains, nose wrinkled, hard gaze aimed at Jacob. "I'm going to bed. Y'all can figure out the sleeping arrangements."

Hayden flees the kitchen and stomps up the stairs, Jacob's gaze fixed firmly on his back. The tension in the room disappears, but Jacob's shoulders are still up to his ears, his strong jaw hard and tense.

"We'll talk tomorrow," Jacob says as he aims a steely look my way, but the words were clearly meant for his brother.

"Nothing to talk about." Parker bumps his fist against Jacob's shoulder. "It's all right, Jake."

Jacob grunts in disagreement, then quietly heads up the stairs like everyone else. Parker looks back at me with a sigh and nods toward my tea. "Finish your tea, then I'll show you up to my room."

"No way," I argue. "I'll sleep on the couch."

Parker rolls his eyes. "Do as I say."

His order rankles me a little, but I don't fight him. Instead, I finish my tea, finally pushing away from the island as a clear indicator that I'm ready for him to show me to bed. Parker takes a moment to clean our mugs before guiding me up the stairs. All the rooms are dark, no light filtering through the spaces at the bottom, even Reid's room.

When our parents had just died, I'd slept outside Reid's bedroom on the floor just in case he'd ever needed me. Of course, he hadn't, because Reid is made of steel and stardust, but maybe I'd needed it more. The proximity to Reid had eased a lot of the initial ache inside me after our parents' deaths. I'll never know if it did anything for him, or if he even knew I did it.

Parker pushes through the final door. "This is my room."

It's very utilitarian. Gray walls, a black metal king-size bed, and a matching dresser. Not many personal items except for a fancy-looking computer setup in the corner. There's a picture on the desk of Parker as a young boy beside Jacob. Back then they almost looked identical, much more so than they do now. But that's it. If I didn't know better, I'd think the room was in a hotel.

Parker heads toward the bed and starts to strip it as I stand frozen.

"What are you—"

"I'm putting clean sheets on the bed for you."

I flush at the thought of him being so considerate. I stand there like the awkward idiot I am, shifting from foot to foot as he quickly remakes the bed with clean sheets and a clean comforter that he grabbed from the walk-in closet on the other side of the room. Once he's finished, he steps away with his hands planted on his hips and tosses me an unsure smile.

"Good?"

"Yeah. Yeah, Parker. Thank you."

"I have an extra toothbrush—"

"I need clothes—"

We both stop when we realize we spoke at the same time. I can feel the flush rise on my cheeks, and my neck heats. Parker just chuckles and takes a small step closer, his moss-green gaze sweeping over my face like a caress. What would it be like to touch him? Not that he'd want that—he's Parker—but sometimes I think about touching someone, anyone, and allowing myself to feel without the fear of germs. To kiss and hold without fear is my greatest life's wish. Well, that and for Reid to stop hating me.

"I have some freshly washed clothes for you, just stay there," Parker orders, as if I'm considering going anywhere but here. He digs around in his dresser for a moment, returning with a well-worn T-shirt and a pair of sweatpants that'll surely swim on me.

Pointing toward the bathroom, I awkwardly ask, "Can I just...?"

"Yeah, go on. Spare toothbrush is under the sink." Parker waves his arm toward the door. "I'll just... wait out here."

I feel myself flush. "Okay."

The bathroom is just as bland and basic as the bedroom. Subway tiles in the shower, dark granite counters, and marble tiles. Even the towels are white. Where is Parker's personality? Everything is so... plain. I look under the sink to find the basket with toothbrushes and tiny tubes of toothpaste. At least that's safe for me. Once I've finished my bedtime routine and dressed in the gigantic shirt and sweatpants, I step back into the bedroom.

Parker has made a pallet on the ground with the dirty comforter and sheets to sleep on. He smiles his reassuring smile again, the one that makes it hard for my anxiety to spin a web of vicious thoughts in my brain. His gaze sweeps over me and his eyebrows pinch together at the sight of me in his clothes. Ugh.

"Yeah, I'll buy you something new to replace these."

Parker looks affronted at the very idea. "Why?"

"Well, I've worn them..."

Parker clears his throat, Adam's apple bobbing hard. "That's not a problem. It's fine. I'm going to go get ready for bed now."

I climb into the soft bed, my eyes already growing heavy just from the cloudy softness beneath me. I don't know why I assumed his bed would be hard, maybe because of the blandness of his room. But the bed is pleasantly soft, like sleeping on a fluffy cloud. The sheets and comforter smell like lavender, comforting me and making me drowsy. Parker steps out of the bathroom in just sweatpants, and my mouth goes dry at the sight. He's on the thinner side, but his muscles are made for quickness, tight and beautiful. I glance away from him to control my reaction. The light goes off a second later, and the room is tossed into pitch blackness. All I can hear is the sound of Parker curling up in the makeshift bed on the floor at the foot of the bed.

"Good night, Mason," Parker calls out, hesitant and tired sounding.

"Good night, Parker."

But I kind of wish he'd call me Mace again. What will I have to do to earn that?

CHAPTER 5

PARKER

I tossed and turned all night. Every time Mason would shift, make a little snuffling noise, or just fucking exist, my body would go on full alert. Even now, as the sun slits through the bottom of my blackout curtains, my body is aware of him in a way it's never been before. I've only ever felt this protective over Jacob, and even then, not this kind of protectiveness.

I rub my sternum, not sure what that feeling in my chest is still. Last night, when I'd watched him kill his uncle, watched the fear blossom across his face, I'd had this unrelenting need to make sure he was okay. Not just safe from the repercussions from his actions, but make sure he didn't hurt inside.

The sound of Jacob cooking downstairs filters into the bedroom, which in turn appears to slowly wake Mason from his deep slumber. I watch out of the corner of my eye as he stretches under the blankets and has a jaw-cracking yawn. He appears to remember where he is, because he squeezes his eyes tightly, slowly lifting the blankets to his nose to breathe in deeply. Oh. I quickly look away and squeeze my own eyes shut in pretend sleep. The bed trembles as he climbs out, then he carefully steps over me to head toward the bathroom.

The sound of the shower turning on does something to me I can't explain. Mason using my shower... Mason naked. *Oh my god, Parker, stop imagining your friend naked.* Because Mason's my friend. I don't have any friends besides Dante. I don't let anyone close enough to be my friend.

I'm sweating and near a panic attack by the time Mason wanders out of the bathroom with wet hair, still wearing my clothes from the night before. He has a scar on his left bicep, thick and surgical in appearance. What is it from? Mason must feel my stare because he glances over his shoulder as he inspects my desk. He looks shy, maroon splashing across his cheeks, almost the same shade as his dark auburn hair.

"Morning," Mason says shyly.

"Morning," I echo, voice huskier than I've ever heard it.

"It sounds like breakfast downstairs?"

I nod slowly as I sit up. "That's Jacob. He's the cook."

"I remember... from when Reid was missing."

"Right." I roll to a stand and look back at Mason, only to catch him turning away to stare at the door like it holds all the secrets of the universe. "Wanna go see if there's any more news? And get some breakfast."

"Sure," Mason replies, but he sounds anything but sure.

I grab a hoodie from my desk chair and tug it on, then lead Mason down the stairs. Jacob must be cooking waffles because Hayden is snarking loudly at him. Hayden is very particular about his waffles.

"You're going to burn them," Hayden hisses from beside Jacob.

Jacob just sends an amused look his way. "How often have I burned your waffles, boss?"

That only seems to infuriate Hayden further, which is pretty typical for them. I make enough noise they hear us both shuffling in. Jacob glances at me over his shoulder, nods, then returns to his cooking. No Dante and Reid yet, so I pull a chair out for Mason, kindly pushing it in for him once he's at the table. I ignore Jacob and Hayden's muffled arguing. Instead, I focus on making myself a cup of coffee and a cup of black tea for Mason.

Back at the table, I put a little milk and sugar into my coffee, then settle in the chair beside Mason. The kitchen is warm from Jacob's cooking, and the light outside is that soft winter yellow that promises a chilly day. Hopefully today is calmer than yesterday, and hopefully we get some good news.

"Hey, Eastport is on CNN right now," Dante announces as he swaggers into the kitchen, heading straight for the plate of sausages sitting invitingly on the island. He grabs one, takes a bite, then turns around with a shit-eating grin. "You will never *guess* what happened overnight."

"No, I won't guess, so please just tell me," I reply dryly.

Dante looks a little put out but just shrugs while hastily fixing himself breakfast. Jacob goes to swat him since it's obviously not ready, but he expertly dodges Jacob after years of practice. I fight the urge to chuckle. Dante grabs a hot waffle from the plate and dodges away from Hayden to join us at the table.

"They found Senator Warton's body... down by the river."

Hayden abruptly turns around. "*What?*"

"Yeah," Dante answers around a mouthful of sausage. "I guess he was mugged."

"I don't understand..." Mason looks around the room at everyone, cheeks flushed. "But I killed him."

Jacob waves the spatula at Mason to make a point. "Nuh-uh, my dude, he was *mugged* by the *riverfront*, and that's the story we all need to stick to for like the rest of forever."

Mason looks so confused, I have to hold back a laugh. After years of all this, I've gotten used to rolling with the punches. Like Reid said last night, it really is always freaking something.

Jacob makes both me and Mason a plate, setting them down on the table in front of us. A moment later, a pink-cheeked Reid strolls into the kitchen. Mason watches his brother make a cup of orange juice with an amused, tender sort of look on his face. The way Mason looks at Reid speaks of so much love. Do I ever look at Jacob that way? I love my twin, but I cannot imagine looking at him like cotton candy shoots out of his ears.

"Morning," Reid greets everyone.

"And?" Dante presses.

Reid narrows his eyes. "I am sorry about the tantrum last night."

"We're used to it by now," Jacob teases while taking his own seat at the table.

Hayden is last because he has to pour approximately thirty-two ounces of syrup all over his waffles, much to Jacob's combined chagrin and fond annoyance.

"So... we just accept the fact that my uncle's body was seemingly moved and made to look like he was mugged?" Mason asks, voice tinged with a hint of sarcasm. I kind of like it a little, when he gets sassier. It proves his walls around us are lowering.

Hayden grunts as he shovels a huge bite of waffle into his mouth. "Yesh, just go widdet."

Jacob turns to glare at Hayden. "What?"

Hayden rolls his eyes, swallows, then turns back to Mason. "Just go with it. What's the worst that could happen?"

Mason visibly blanches. "So many things. Do not ask a person with anxiety a question like that."

"Hmmm, well. We'll figure it out. I still think Parker moving into your house isn't a bad idea, in case this all goes tits up."

"Great!" Mason says again with obvious forced enthusiasm.

Hayden grins lecherously. "Glad you're so excited. Welcome to the family."

Reid sighs, that sigh he always lets out when we're all being particularly us. "Mason, it'll be fine. At least we don't have to deal with Marc anymore. That's the positive."

"Yeah, I guess," Mason grumbles. He pushes around the waffle on his plate instead of eating it.

"It's really good," I murmur out of the corner of my mouth.

Mason sneaks a look at me, then angrily stabs the waffle, taking a hesitant bite. Something hot and decidedly weird blooms in my belly while watching Mason make himself eat. The other boys are quiet during the majority of breakfast, save for a few delighted moans at how good Jacob's food always is. Once done, I grab Mason's mostly cleared plate and head over to the sink to help Reid with the dishes.

"No." Reid shakes his head and looks sheepish, which is odd for him. "I, uh, I have dishes for the next week."

"But we usually do them together..."

Reid clears his throat and grimaces. "Listen, just... I'm washing dishes for the week, okay?"

I shrug because I don't really care to argue. When I turn back around, Dante's got his eyes firmly on Reid, a look of fond pride in his eyes. Oh yuck. Mason's staring down at his nails like they're the most interesting thing in the world, probably to avoid watching his brother and Dante's odd dynamic.

"I'll pack a bag, then we can head over to your house, if you want?"

Mason looks up at me, unsure, but nods all the same. "Yeah, thank you. I like your house but..."

I smile down at him. "Nothing like your own house. I get it."

Mason nods again, a flush working its way across his cheeks. Hayden snorts from across the table, and when I glance over, he rolls his eyes and makes a *jerking off* motion. Narrowing my eyes at him, I make a *shooting myself in the head* motion then point at him. Jacob snorts at us, then crumbles under the fury of Hayden's gaze.

I leave them be and head up to my room to pack. I toss all the necessary daily stuff into a duffel bag, including my gun safe, then put a few mission-ready suits into a garment bag. Grabbing my rifle from the wall in my walk-in closet, I double-check the safety is on, put it into its soft case, and sling it over my shoulder.

"Ready to go?" I call out to Mason the moment my feet hit the first floor.

Mason turns to look at me, then back to Reid, who is still dutifully washing dishes. He nods hurriedly but pauses when he stands. Almost as if second-guessing himself, he heads over to Reid and whispers something to him. Reid turns toward Mason with a soft smile and reaches up a bubble-covered hand to tap his own nose. Mason grins warmly before copying the movement with his own finger.

Once the car is packed and Mason is loaded into the passenger seat, I climb in and start it up. It's so freaking cold out, I toggle with the heat to get it to blasting.

"What was the finger thing about?" I ask curiously.

Mason flushes. "It's this thing we developed when we were little to say we love one another."

That's cute. "Can I ask you something?"

The bright light of a chilly morning assaults us when I back out of the garage. Mason twists his fingers in my too-large shirt, his lips twisting up as if he's afraid I'm going to ask him a question he doesn't have the answer to.

"Yeah, I guess…"

"It's about your OCD."

Mason looks relieved. "Yeah, that's okay. It's a part of me, so I don't get embarrassed by it."

"Did that start young?"

Mason nods and turns his head to look out the window, effectively hiding his gaze from me. Instead of staring at him, I decide to focus on the road, my hands reflexively tightening on the steering wheel.

"Yeah. I had acute lymphocytic leukemia, or what's commonly referred to as ALL, as a kid. I was around eight when I was diagnosed. I guess I just got sick and didn't get better, then I started having the telltale signs of leukemia, so it all snowballed. I had to get a bone marrow transplant, and because of some risk factors, I was, like, medium risk? I don't know, I can't remember everything." Mason sounds resigned, face still turned away so I can't see him. "My mother went a little over the top. After I was in remission, she still kept me out of school and kept me away from *risky activities*. My immune system took a while to rebound after all the treatments."

"What are risky activities?"

Mason snorts and his face twists in anger when he glances back at me. "Anything that involved leaving the house basically. She just did too much. Looking back, I think she had OCD too, she just hyper-focused on me because she was so convinced any small childhood illness would now kill me. Going off to college was a hard-fought battle, but once I turned eighteen, she couldn't really control me anymore. By then Reid was already acting out for our parents' attention. I just wanted to get away for once."

"I get it."

Mason turns to look at me, his gaze steely. "Do you?"

I grip the steering wheel tighter, swallowing hard. "Yeah, it was just Jacob and me a lot. We had a single mom, and she worked nonstop. She cared about us, but she was never there, not like she needed to be. So it was Jacob and I against the world for a lot of things. Yeah, she fed us, kept us safe, put clothes on our backs, but we kind of raised each other."

"Is that why you both act like feral alley cats sometimes?"

I snort a laugh and can't help but smirk. "Yeah, probably. She died when we were teens. She'd smoked a pack a day since she was young, and it caught up to her. After that, we really did raise each other. We ended up in separate foster homes, then found our way to a group home. When we turned eighteen, we gained access to the little bit of money from her life insurance and made our way to college."

"It sucked, but I'm glad I was older when our parents died. But taking care of a teen Reid was not easy." Mason laughs sarcastically, then eyes me out of the corner of his eye. "He was and always will be a little shit."

"I believe that," I say truthfully. "Is the scar from your cancer treatments?"

Mason glances down to look at the scar on his bicep with furrowed brows. "Yeah. I had to have a port for a little while. I didn't have good veins, so it was a whole thing. I forget about it sometimes."

"Ah."

"You noticed it though," Mason points out with an air of surprise.

I swallow hard. "It's my job to notice the little things."

Mason just hums and leans back in the seat, sighing in relief when we pull up in front of his house. The drive is short, but it's cold out, and I wouldn't feel comfortable if I didn't have easy access to the car. Mason presses a few buttons on his phone and the small garage in the basement opens up, and he points in that direction for me to pull in.

"You guys don't have a car?"

Mason shrugs in denial. "Neither of us like to drive."

"Fair."

Mason hops out when the garage door is firmly closed and makes his way inside. After grabbing all my stuff, I follow him, relaxing a little bit at the familiar homey feeling of the house. It smells clean like usual, with a hint of lemons.

"I'll show you to the guest room," Mason declares, looking oddly nervous.

"Is it close to your room?" I ask, voice huskier than I intended.

Mason looks up at me through his auburn eyelashes, that glorious flush working its way across his cheeks. "Across the hallway."

I grunt in acceptance. "Okay. You can't be on the first floor without me though."

"But this is my house and I feel perfectly safe here. Also, you have the extra security and—"

"Hey."

Mason's eyes go wide as he stares at me in question.

"You'll stay on the same floor as me always, got it?" I order, leaving no room for arguments.

His shoulders drop from around his ears as he nods in acceptance of my order. He's so different from Reid personality-wise, but I think there's still that spark of fight in him. Mason just doesn't like to push it, which works for me. I want to protect him and keep him safe without him questioning my every damn move.

I follow closely behind Mason as we climb the stairs. The door to his room is closed, but he opens the door across from it and steps inside. I take in the dark blue walls, dark wood bed frame, and muted light-yellow comforter, and something inside me gentles at the sight. Mason is so soft behind his walls. No wonder I have such an urge to protect him, when he deserves protecting the most.

"The bathroom is through that door," Mason says quietly while pointing at the other side of the room. "If you need anything, let me know and I'll order it from the delivery service I use."

"I packed anything I could need."

Mason smiles, but it doesn't reach his eyes. "Even so, I kind of owe you for this, so if you need anything, it's on me."

What's he talking about? Owing me? We're practically family now... and I'm only doing what I'd do for anyone else. I'd protect anyone like this if it was needed. I think. I'm mostly sure, at least.

"Mace, you don't owe me anything," I say to reassure him.

Mason's breath catches for a moment before he glances away from me to stare at the bed hard, like it's personally offended him. "Okay. Well, just, whatever. If you need something, tell me. I'm going to go shower again and put some of my own clothes on now. I'll see you... in a bit."

I almost tell him not to because I want him to stay in my clothes, I want him to smell like me, but he's gone before I can utter a single word. What the fuck is going on with me? I distract myself from thoughts of Mason, the sounds of his shower running, by unpacking all of my belongings into the dresser and hanging my mission-ready clothes into the closet. I keep my rifle in its case and stow it under the bed for easy access, at least until I need it next.

Since my door is open, the sound of Mason's door reopening echoes through my own room. I lean back on my heels to see him standing in his doorway, hair delightfully wet, making it look more bloodred than auburn. He's wearing these tight exercise pants and a baggy T-shirt that has a logo on it that I don't recognize.

I point at his shirt in question. "What's that?"

"Oh." Mason blushes furiously. "It's from *The Goonies*."

"The what?"

Mason blinks and shakes his head, as if totally astounded at my question. "*The Goonies*... It's a movie."

"I'm not much of a movie guy."

"Oh. Well. All right."

"But we can watch it so I can see why you like it."

That gorgeous blush I'm really starting to enjoy splashes across Mason's cheeks and down his throat, sneaking under the shirt with *The Goonies* image on it. He mumbles something I can't quite make out, then starts to descend the stairs, but he seems to recall what I'd said earlier and pauses halfway down with his hand tight on the banister.

"Can we go downstairs?" Mason asks, eyes staring daggers into the bottom step. "I need some tea."

"Sure, Mason." I follow behind him like the agreeable guy I am.

My phone dings in my pocket, and I tug it out as I follow behind Mason into the kitchen.

DANTE

Hayden and Jacob are unbearable when you're not here

As if I keep them in line

DANTE

No, but Jacob is too embarrassed for you to see him making constant moon eyes at Hayden

MOON EYES?

DANTE

Oh brother

Forget it

Wait, are you saying…

Jacob wouldn't do that. We have a rule.

DANTE

What fucking rule, my dude?

That we won't get involved with any of the guys in the house

DANTE

...When did you make this rule

It was an agreement we made in the warehouse before even accepting the deal

DANTE

Uhm

Lol

What?

DANTE

No, just... that's kind of funny. I was so hot you had to make a deal to keep your hands off of me?

You are delusional and insane

Also I'm straight

DANTE

Everyone's a little bit gay

What's that mean

DANTE

It means... enjoy your time with Mason. Maybe you'll figure stuff out.

How did you know you liked Reid?

DANTE

When I saw him dancing at the club, I knew I needed to have him, then he puked on my shoes and sealed the deal.

Weirdo

DANTE

Maybe but I'd kill for Reid, in fact I have killed for Reid, and he'd chew through someone's arm to protect me.

Weirdo(s)

DANTE

Bye

Tell Hayden to call me when he has a chance

DANTE

Fine. Bye.

I lift my head from where it's been buried in my phone to find Mason standing uneasily at the stove, patiently waiting for the kettle to finish. There's a tension in his shoulders I hate, that I wish would disappear, but I don't know how to put him at ease in my presence besides doing what I've been doing. I knew how to calm him last night; it's easy when he's too far gone—just talk to him like a skittish horse. But when he's in between too far gone and happy as a clam, it's difficult to find the right thing to say or do to bring him back. I'm always worried I'll misstep somehow and hurt him further.

"What are you worried about?" I ask him softly. Taking a seat at the table, Mason ignores my question to pour the water into mugs, finally dunking tea bags into each cup.

He lets out a pained sigh and slumps down into the chair opposite me, his hands carefully cupped around the mug. "I'm still trying to build those boxes in my head."

Ah. "It gets easier with practice."

I take a sip of the scalding hot tea, then grab the honey that sits in the middle of the dark oak table. Mason watches curiously as I add honey to the tea, and his mouth lifts at the corners slightly in amusement.

"So what's the plan if you have one of your secret missions? Can I stay here alone?"

"Yes, but Hayden will watch the cameras."

"Flawed plan," Mason comments, dancing a delicate finger across the rim of his mug, back and forth. The movement is hypnotizing. "What about when there's a mission and you're *all* in on it."

"You'll go with us and stay in the car like last time."

"You're not going to shove me in the panic room at your place like Dante did to Reid?"

I take a small sip of tea to avoid answering. The panic room had a flaw where it had been possible for someone to use heat on the hand scanner to mimic one of our hands. It's been fixed, and now the panic room only opens with a verbal password that someone can't use a recording to imitate. The new procedure took weeks to test.

"I'll put you in the panic room if I have to," I say cautiously, hoping Mason picks up on the weight of my words. I won't think twice about putting him in there. I'll do anything to protect any of my brothers, and that means Mason by extension. "But if I have a mission, Hayden will watch the cameras. I'll put him on watch duty."

Mason makes a sound that's a mix between a snort and a hum. "I guess you have it all figured out."

"You're sassier than I remember."

Mason closes his eyes on a sigh. "This is how I am once the anxiety starts to ebb. I took a pill after I showered."

I can feel my eyebrows furrow. The look on my face must be one of confusion because Mason chuckles and ruefully shakes his head.

"I take daily medication for my OCD. It helps *a lot*, but I'm not cured. I have weekly therapy to help. It's not fast acting but sometimes just taking the pill makes me feel better." Mason sighs and looks down at the table, looking more tired than I've ever seen him. "Back when it was really bad, I had so many compulsions I almost flunked out of college. It took me an hour to do something that would take another person, like, five minutes. I'm still getting better but..." Mason splays his hands on the table and shrugs. "Work in progress, I guess."

"And the OCD..."

Mason shrugs again. "I definitely think I always had it, but cancer was the first trigger, then my parents dying just... intensified it."

We finish our tea in silence. Despite the homework I need to finish, all the things I could do to double-check the safety of the alarm system I installed, or the way I could count the spray of freckles across Mason's cheeks—I don't do any of that. Instead, I take our mugs to the sink, hand-wash them twice, then put them into the dishwasher.

When I turn back around, Mason is watching me with a confused, but thankful, sort of look. I smile at him, the same smile that calmed him the other night after he'd committed his first murder. Nodding toward the living room, I say, "Show me *The Goonies*?"

Mason's face lights up like the Fourth of July. We move to the living room and settle on the couch, far enough away from each other that we're not touching, but close enough I can feel the heat of him. I can't help but watch him through most of the movie though. Sometimes his lips move with the lines because he has them all memorized, and I find that more endearing than I should. Dangerously so.

CHAPTER 6
PARKER

The next morning, I dress in slacks and a sweater, then haphazardly put my hair up in a half bun at the top of my head. When I descend the stairs with my bag and rifle tossed over my shoulder, Mason is waiting anxiously in the kitchen. He's already broken my rule.

"You're supposed to *always* be on the same floor as me. Remember?"

"Will I be safe here?" Mason asks, voice a little frantic.

I nod, because it seems to lessen his anxiety. "Yeah, this place is Fort Knox. But if you want, I can take you to the house on my way to campus?"

Mason shakes his head furiously. "No, I need to be in my own home." He laughs awkwardly. "Although, I have no work to do now that I'm not hacking for my uncle."

"Do you need a job?"

Mason shrugs. "Not really. We've enough money from the wrongful death settlement to never have to work a day in our lives. Our parents would be happy about that at least, I think."

"Well, I only have two morning classes, then I'll be back. I can talk to Hayden to see if he can use your hacking abilities, but Robin is kind of strict about people helping us unless they've approved of you."

Mason waves his hand in a dismissive way. "Go to class. I'll be here. Not going anywhere."

I take a step forward, to do what I don't know, and Mason takes a step back with wide eyes. We stand awkwardly for a few moments, both unsure of what I was about to do. I sigh, then flee the house to head to school.

What is wrong with me? Jesus. I rub my eyes with one hand while carefully steering with the other. Why did I step forward to touch Mason, attempting to calm him with my touch? When I know he doesn't even *want* to be touched. I'm going crazy. The predictable steadiness of my morning classes slightly calms my already frayed nerves though. By the time I'm done, I feel like I'm going to spiral.

Instead of texting Dante after class, I call him.

"Uhm, are you dying?" Dante asks when he picks up after the first ring. We never call each other, so I don't blame him for being curious.

"No."

"Uh."

"Will you go to the range with me? I need to let off some steam."

"Yeah. Give me ten minutes and I'll wait for you out front. Do you want Jacob to watch over Mason?"

I let out a sigh. "No, he doesn't need it. I'll give access to the security cameras to Hayden so someone can check in every now and then."

"Sure."

And then Dante hangs up. The ten-minute drive to

the house calms me a little more, especially with the promise of going to the range to let off some steam. When I pull up, Dante is waiting outside with a bag slung over his shoulder just as he promised, dressed in all-black with a pair of bright red Chucks on. He slides into the car with a Cheshire grin that immediately sets me on edge.

"The point of this outing is for me to *relax*, not to goad me."

"I never goad anyone," Dante replies, willfully lying through his teeth.

We stare at each other for a few moments until Dante sighs and rolls his eyes. "Okay, I do sometimes, but not you unless you start it. What's this about? Hayden grabbed me on the way out of the house and told me there's a mission tomorrow night, by the way. I'm surprised we're not keeping a low profile considering everything."

"Did Hayden talk to Robin about Mason?"

Dante shrugs, eyes on the road. "Not that I know of, but he keeps all of that so hush-hush. Why do you need to go to the range so badly?" Dante wiggles his eyebrows salaciously. "Got some frustration you need to let out?"

Instead of answering, I gun the engine so that Dante jerks back, then slam hard on the brakes so he jerks forward. The look he sends me is lethal, but I just grin in the face of his fury. That'll teach him a lesson. The range we go to is out in the suburbs, and it's membership only, so there won't be anyone there on a day pass just learning how to handle a gun, like you'll find at a public range. Also, no cops allowed, which is always a plus. We don't need cops sniffing around. Hopping out of the car, I swing my rifle over my shoulder, glad that I stashed it in the car earlier so I didn't have to run back to

Mason's house and explain myself. Not that Mason would ask, but I'd feel the urge to tell him, which is almost worse.

"Reid is still begging me to teach him to shoot," Dante grumbles beside me.

I shoot him a curious look. "I don't know why you won't let him at least have knowledge. What if he's on a mission with us, something goes wrong, and he needs to defend himself? It's only logical to teach him the mechanics at least."

Dante sighs and rubs a tired hand over his face. "I just want to keep him innocent in this *one* single way."

The idea of Reid being innocent in any shape or form sends me into a fit of mild hysterics. I grab Dante's arm to stop him in the parking lot of the range while I bend over with painful laughter. Oh my god, it actually hurts.

"Sorry, that was just so funny." I stand and wipe away pretend tears from my eyes. "Hearing you mention the words innocent and Reid in the same sentence is just fucking hilarious."

Dante rolls his eyes. "You know what I meant. The taser is enough."

"It is certainly not enough," I argue while swinging the door of the range open. "Not when we deal with the kinds of people we deal with."

Dante grumbles something undoubtedly sarcastic behind me that I can't make out. We pass by the sales counters, waving at the normal guys, before using our passes to swipe into the secure back. The stillness of the range settles me. Dante and I pick stalls side by side and go about getting ready. The last stall has a setup for my rifle so that I can get on the ground for sharp shooting, despite the target being at too close a distance to make the practice skillful. Earmuffs first, then eye protection, and then I set about readying the rifle.

"Want to place a bet?" Dante calls out, loud enough to be heard through the ear protection.

I snort as I lie down on the ground on my stomach, setting my rifle up. Ignoring him will only fuel him on.

"I don't want to embarrass you," I shout back, just before leaning down to adjust my sights.

The target is in view, and I take a deep breath, pulling the trigger as I release the inhale. Right in the center. Perfect. Dante's predictable pops rend the air as he shoots less for aim and more for maximum damage. Since the room is empty, I go about moving around to take aim at all the targets scattered down the concrete wall. Dante's shots quiet as he no doubt watches me angle until I've hit the mark on all ten targets.

Rolling over onto my back, I stare up at Dante standing over me with his arms crossed. Grumpy and sullen, just the way I'm used to him.

"You've always got to show me up."

"Your skills lie elsewhere," I tell him, meaning every single word.

The corner of his mouth lifts in a hint of a smile. We pack up the guns, careful to ensure they're properly stored, before heading out of the range. The air outside is pleasantly chilly after working up a sweat in the heat of the range. We settle into the car quietly, mutually deciding to skip lunch.

"Does Reid talk about Mason much?" I ask, trying to sound casual, sound *cool*. But per usual, Dante notices my question exactly for what it is.

Dante chuckles soft and low while sending me an *I see through your bullshit* sort of look.

"Oh, Parker, Parker, Parker."

"Cut it out," I say with an annoyed groan.

"I don't think I will actually." Dante tosses me a scary, gleeful smile. "Why yes, Reid does speak about Mason. Mostly in a glowing sort of way."

I clear my throat awkwardly, keeping my eyes firmly on the road as I drive us back home. "Has he ever dated before?"

"Mason?"

"Shut up. I'm trying to gauge... things."

"He's not dated that Reid is aware of but that doesn't say much. They had a really tense relationship for a few years."

I nod because I at least knew that much. Dante is unusually quiet the rest of the ride. When we pull up to the house, I go to jump out to be social, but Dante lays a firm hand on my arm.

"Mason needs a gentle hand," Dante murmurs softly.

I stare at him in confusion. "What's that even mean?"

"I mean that he just killed his uncle, his parents died in a traumatic fashion from an airplane crash, and he is a childhood cancer survivor."

Now, I'm irritated. "What are you saying?"

Dante removes his hand and scratches at his slightly stubbled cheek. For the first time I notice the lack of bags beneath his eyes, how his hair is cut a little shorter to highlight the way it slightly curls at the ends. He looks better—happier—since he's been with Reid. Maybe being in love has done him good.

"I'm saying you can be a bit of a playboy, and Mason doesn't need that energy. He doesn't need you figuring yourself out with him."

I glare at Dante hard enough to have him shrinking back a little in the car. "I'm not a playboy. I hook up way less than you used to and only when I have an itch. I can't help it that I get unwanted attention."

"No, I know that, Parker..."

"Then what?"

Dante rubs a hand over his face again, then hops out of the car. He dips down to look at me, this time pinning me with his hard gaze. I've stared down scarier men and shot them between the eyes, so his look really does nothing to scare me. But it does remind me that I can't be impulsive when it comes to Mason. I've got to figure out these feelings myself before I approach him with them. No matter how much Mason with wet hair, barefoot, and a shy gaze makes my insides squirm with some emotion I can't name.

"Just give it time, Parker. Give it time."

And then Dante disappears inside without another word. I decide to avoid dealing with the other guys and head back toward Mason's house. The house smells like cleaning chemicals when I step inside. Not in the pleasant way where someone just cleaned their house, but in a way that seems like someone used entire bottles to clean each room.

I toe off my shoes on the mat by the front door. "Fuck."

I go through each room until I find Mason cleaning the upstairs guest bathroom, on his hands and knees, wearing yellow gloves and an industrial mask over his face. We stare at each other for a few fraught moments before Mason bends forward to rest his forehead against the ground, effectively making him let go of the soaked sponge.

"Mason..."

"I'm sorry," Mason cries, shoulders shaking.

Fuck. I want to touch him, hold him. I don't know how else to show that I care or that I'm here without physical touch. But I've got to learn. It's a long game here.

"Is it okay if I sit?" I ask quietly.

Mason sniffles and lifts his head slightly to watch me lower to the ground. Sitting crisscross-applesauce, I rest my hands on my knees to hopefully portray that I come in peace. I tilt my head as I look at him.

"Can you sit up too so I can look at you?"

Mason sniffles again, sounding so pitiful my heart breaks for him. He sits up, but all I can see are the sweaty strands of his hair and the piercing blue of his eyes due to the mask.

"What happened?"

Mason visibly grimaces even beneath the mask. "I just couldn't box it up in my head like you said. I kept thinking and thinking and *thinking*, and the only way to silence it was to clean."

"Did you take some medicine?"

Mason shakes his head. "I didn't want to. I wasn't triggered, I just... I'm scared. I don't know how all of you stay so calm. I mean, I killed a man! My uncle! And then someone fucking moved his body and made it look like he was mugged. What the fuck?"

I nod, which he accepts as understanding. "You're right, it's all really fucked up. But I promised you that you won't go to prison and I stand by that. Even if something comes out, I won't let you go, okay?"

"But how?" Mason cries, close to hysterical.

"Just trust me. You trusted me the other night, to get you home, to keep you safe. Trust me when I tell you that everything's going to be okay."

Mason takes some gasping breaths, his fingers working against the ground like he's trying to hold on to the side of a glacier. "God, I can't breathe in here anymore."

I stand quickly and gesture for him to copy me. "Let's go outside."

We make our way out to the back porch. I take a grateful gulp of the fresh air. We're going to have to open every window for the afternoon to get the chemical smell out of the house. But we'll make do, I guess.

Mason tiredly slumps down into one of the wrought iron chairs. I sit beside him, grimacing at the feel of the cold metal seeping through my thin shirt. Mason whips the mask off, and I finally catch a good look at his face. His cheeks are red from the exertion of cleaning and his lips look chapped. He swipes his tongue across his lips, and sudden vertigo hits me when I overheat, my pulse pounding hard in my chest like I'm being chased by a dinosaur. Fuck. Holy shit.

I'm attracted to Mason.

And I decide to have this epiphany when he's having a grade A–level anxiety attack.

I am an astonishingly awful person.

"Maybe... Maybe you need to kill another person?" I ask hesitantly.

Mason turns his horror-struck gaze toward me. "I'm sorry. I think I misheard you."

"Hear me out..."

Mason shakes his head so furiously it looks painful. "Parker. No, oh my god. I'm going to go into cardiac arrest."

"Can I touch you?"

My question stills Mason. His chest calms its rapid movements and his eyes catch on mine. "No. No, but... I wish you could."

I guess that's good enough. I lean closer to him, wishing he could allow me to touch him, to calm him with a firm hand on his thigh or brush away the sweaty auburn strands of hair that stick to his forehead.

"Listen. Maybe killing someone else will help because then it won't be just your uncle. I don't know, I can run it by the guys."

Mason takes a deep breath and tiredly tilts his head back to stare listlessly up at the sky. I try not to get caught up in the sight of his throat bobbing, but it's impossible. Now that the train has left the station, I can't keep the thoughts from running rampant. What would he taste like? What would he sound like if I kissed the hollow of his throat? What does he smell like in the mornings after a night of deep sleep? And could I hold him all night to keep his terrifying thoughts at bay? I'm so beyond screwed.

Mason ends up laughing, still slightly hysterical, but free from the grips of panic. "I can't exactly run it by my therapist either. *Hey, Nora, I killed my uncle and now I'm wondering if killing another person will make me stop thinking about going to prison?*"

I grin at Mason, unable to hold my own laughter back. "It's just a thought."

Mason sighs deeply, then aims his tortured deep blue gaze at me. "Has Reid killed someone yet?"

I shake my head. "No, Dante won't let him."

"Won't let him?" Mason echoes, frowning.

"It's a line Dante has. He wants to keep Reid innocent."

That startles another laugh out of Mason, and suddenly we're both laughing like school kids. It's so nice just to laugh with him. When I'm with him I don't feel like I have to be *cool* or be the perfect shot like I am with the boys, I can just be... me. Just Parker. Once the laughter fades, Mason takes a deep, strained breath. The chilly air washes over us and

Mason looks back at the house with an exhausted air about him.

"I'll go open up the windows to air the place out. You stay here," I order him, feeling the need to take care of this one thing for him.

Mason doesn't reply, nor does he move when I curl my hand around the back of his chair in the imitation of a touch. Flexing my fingers as I walk toward the house, I look back in hopes that he's watching me. But Mason is just looking forward, head held high.

I tug out my phone as I walk around the house and open the windows to air out the chemicals Mason almost killed us with.

> I want to bring Mason on the next group mission. I want him to participate.

HAYDEN

> Closed invites only.

> I'm fucking serious.

HAYDEN

> I decide who comes on missions and the team is closed.

> Don't make me pull rank, boss.

Hayden goes silent, which I know means he's seething. I can picture his nostrils flaring and his fingers clenching his phone tight enough to smash it. I pause at Mason's bedroom door. Is going into his bedroom an invasion of his privacy? Oh well. I decide to risk it and push into his room. It's different than I expected. Bright light-blue walls, cream curtains, and a fluffy pale yellow bedspread. His bedroom feels like being in the sky. But it still smells like lemon chemical cleaner, so I open the window that overlooks the backyard.

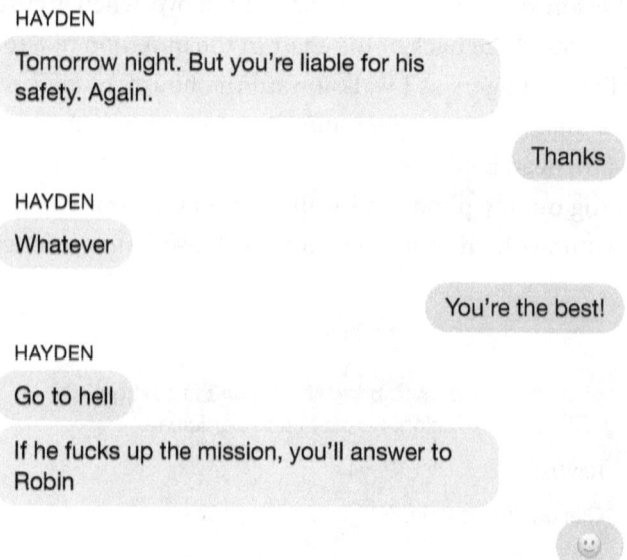

HAYDEN

Tomorrow night. But you're liable for his safety. Again.

Thanks

HAYDEN

Whatever

You're the best!

HAYDEN

Go to hell

If he fucks up the mission, you'll answer to Robin

Mason is still sitting outside when I come back downstairs. His head is tipped back against the chair, tilted toward the sky, eyes firmly shut. What is he thinking? Sometimes Mason is so easy to understand, yet often he's still a firmly shut book. How long will it take me to learn his tells like he's so easily starting to learn mine?

"You're going to come with us two days from now," I say.

Mason blinks slowly up at me like Scully does when she's awoken from a very pleasant nap.

"Coming with you where?" Mason asks, curiosity coloring his voice.

I shrug because I don't know where yet. "On the mission."

"Parker..."

I hold a hand out to ask for him to listen. "Just *trust* me, Mason. Okay?"

Mason finally just nods and leans his head back again with a sigh. "I trust you."

Those three little words shouldn't mean as much to me as they do.

CHAPTER 7

MASON

W hat the hell was I thinking? My muscles still ache from scrubbing the entire house clean two days ago. Everything aches like I ran five marathons back-to-back. But I'm practicing building those boxes in my head—indestructible boxes that make it impossible for those scary thoughts to escape. Those frightening memories are locked away where they can't hurt me, where I can't hurt myself.

A knock on my door startles me while I'm lying supine, attempting to practice my breathing techniques. Absolutely no anxiety about tonight. None! Nothing bad will happen. Likely.

"Come in," I call out, leaning up on my elbows.

Parker opens the door enough to peek his head through. "I've got something for you."

I sit up on the bed, eagerly waiting for him to come inside. I love presents but hate surprises. Parker's strides toward me are sure and steady, but his hands shake a little as he pulls a medium-sized black box from behind his back.

"I got you some mission gear. We have someone who

stocks clothes for us, and I pulled a little favor to get it ready so quick," Parker admits with a hint of embarrassment. "But you don't have to wear it if you don't want to."

Wow. Why does he look so embarrassed? "Oh cool, let me see."

Parker tightly hugs the box to his chest for a second. "The thing is, all of us dress differently, wearing what feels comfortable for us. Dante wears traditional mission clothes, and so does Jacob, but Hayden... He wears... It's more club-wear kind of. Reid is dressed like Dante because they're a couple." Parker pauses as if caught in a huge mistake. He clears his throat and aims his dark green eyes down at the box in his hand. "Well, I got you some gear from where I bought mine. If that's fine."

He still won't look at me, which is so polar opposite of his normal personality. Parker so often calms me when I need it most. I now feel the same need deep in the pit of my belly. To calm him, reassure him that this show of vulnerability with me is okay in the soft stillness of my bedroom.

"Let me see, Parker," I tell him tenderly.

Parker's eyes flit up to mine as a smile lifts up the corner of his lips. "Okay."

He sets the box on the ground and opens it up. One by one, he tugs out what looks like a bespoke outfit made just for me.

"I'll have more made for you if you like it."

The shirt is long sleeve and black, but with a shimmer to it that makes it look like it was dusted with a layer of glitter. The pants are midnight black without any shimmer and skinny, obviously meant to hug my legs tightly. There's also a halter made in what looks like supple brand-new black leather, with shiny oxford shoes to match. But the shoes aren't normal dress shoes. I can tell the inside is made for comfort, and the tips have an odd dome to them.

"They're steel-toed," Parker explains as he notices my curious look toward the shoes.

"Oh."

"Do you want to put it on? I had my tailor use materials that are soft against your skin, and I've washed it with your preferred detergent."

I curl my fingers into my palm so hard it stings. I will probably succumb to the attention Parker lavishes on me one day. Of course, he won't do it on purpose, but I'm falling for him harder and faster each time he does something thoughtful.

I stand abruptly from the bed, and Parker moves back a little to give me the space he always so attentively gives. I hold my hand out in demand for the clothes. I can't spend one more second in his presence without saying something stupid like *kiss me, but I've never been kissed and it might gross me out and send me into a panic attack.* I've spent so many years dreaming of being kissed—of that perfect first kiss—that the idea of having it but reacting badly could send me into a spiral all on its own.

After Parker gingerly hands me the clothes, I disappear into the bathroom to put on my new mission aesthetic. I avoid the mirror as I dress, running my hands down the buttoned shirt and over my thighs. The clothes fit me like a glove, like someone poured them over my body so they fit just right. The holster is a little more difficult as I slip it over my arms. Turning to look in the mirror, a startled gasp rattles around the room at the image that greets me.

I look... hot. I run my fingers through my hair, attempting in vain to make it lie in a way that gives off the same vibes as the outfit. But it's a fruitless endeavor because my hair is my hair, no matter what I do. I lost my hair during chemo as a kid, and once it grew back, it came back with a curl, unruly no matter how much I attempt to tame it.

When I step into the bedroom, Parker spins around and his jaw clenches hard, the muscles working at the hinges. His eyes get stuck on my thighs, so I glance down, but I have no idea what he's seeing.

"Is it okay?" I ask, suddenly shy.

Parker grunts, then clears his throat a couple of times. "Yeah. It fits well? Do you need me to tighten the holster? I can do it without touching you... probably."

I smile at him. "I think it's okay. Are you giving me a gun?"

Parker nods, throat bobbing on a swallow. "Yeah, one of Hayden's."

"Oh. Not one of yours?"

Parker's smirk warms me to the bone. "I usually only carry the tranquilizer gun if I'm not using the rifle. I'm giving you a *real* gun."

"Oh." It's just hitting me that tonight I'm likely going to kill someone. Again.

"We can cancel all this if you don't want to go through with it. You still have time to change your mind." Parker's eyes flit between mine, a careful caress without touch. "But I've thought about this a lot, and I think it would help, in an insane sort of way. It helps me... to kill sometimes. So anyway..."

Oh. Parker is so genuine with his answer that my heart races a little bit. There are so many nuances to him I've yet to meet, I could probably spend a long time charting a path through to discover.

"No!" I shout, but I soften my voice when his eyes widen.

"No. I want to do it. I'm not changing my mind. I'm just getting nervous, which is my standard level of emotion. There's nervous, then there's anxiety attack, then there's the panic. Nervous is fine."

Parker looks at me almost... fondly. "All right then, let's go."

I take a deep breath as I follow Parker down the stairs, trying *very* hard not to look at his ass in his own bespoke outfit. Parker helps me into the passenger seat like usual, then dips down a little to look me in the eye. He seems excited.

"I forgot the best part." Parker reaches into his back pocket and pulls out a pair of leather gloves. "This way you shouldn't get triggered if you have to touch something. Plus, no prints left behind."

I touch the supple leather with a soft smile. "Oh."

"By the way, Jacob usually sits here, so you might get some ribbing. Just ignore them all."

I blink slowly at him. "Okay. Jacob can sit here..."

Parker shakes his head furiously. "Nope, no one will touch you up here."

Then Parker slams the door with finality. Oh. Does he mean that for my OCD or does he mean that because he doesn't want anyone touching me? Anyone that isn't him. I watch him out of the corner of my eye as he pulls out of the driveway to head toward the other house. His lightly muscled arms bunch as he turns the car, making that helpless young gay man inside me want to scream. Why are arms so sexy?

Parker puts on some grunge-sounding rock music, then flicks me a smile. "Nolan Hastings, I love him."

"I'm more of a pop guy."

"Don't worry, you'll learn." Parker shoots me a devastating

smile before turning the music up. The guy's voice is deep, reminiscent of singers from the early nineties. Parker taps the steering wheel along with the beat, his mouth softly mouthing the lyrics as well. That's kind of sexy too.

The door to the house swings open the minute we pull up front. Dante holds the door open for Reid, who is dressed like his boyfriend, like Parker said, and then Hayden and Jacob follow. How are they all going to fit? My question is answered when Jacob opens the door for Hayden, who slides into the middle seat like it was made for him. Dante and Jacob flank him, then Reid clamors in straight onto Dante's lap. That cannot be safe. If we stop at a red light beside a cop, we're definitely going to get a ticket, which will blow the entire mission.

"Is that safe—"

"Well, I'd have a seat if you weren't joining us," Reid interrupts me with a steely edge to his voice.

I turn around to glare at him. "Parker invited me, so take it up with him if you don't want me here."

Dante digs his fingers into Reid's arms, which seems to simultaneously calm and frustrate Reid further. But he shuts up all the same. I don't even know what the damn mission is for. Or protocol. Sweat starts to dampen the back of my neck, but when I look toward Parker, he shoots me a reassuring smile that I feel all the way in my bones. Parker won't let anything bad happen to me, and he won't let me mess up.

Parker pulls off the highway thirty minutes later, dumping us straight into the suburbs. The bright lights of the city have faded. Moonshine guides our way as the streetlights are placed farther and farther apart. My anxiety mutes a little at the thrill of the mission that's about to unfold before us. Maybe killing bad guys is therapeutic?

Finally, Parker pulls into a dark industrial center, only the light of the moon guiding our way to a deserted parking lot. Despite the barren surroundings, Parker parks the car at the back of the lot, closest to the exit. Hayden leans forward in the dark of the car with a plucky smile that sends a shiver of trepidation down my spine.

"Welcome to the shit show," Hayden sings. Jacob elbows him in the ribs, which makes Hayden shoot the other man a glare. "Fuck off, Jacob. Now listen up, perky. Parker is responsible for you on this one, so if you blow it, I'll punish Parker for at *least* a month by putting him on protection duty for me, which is his least favorite duty."

What? I shake my head at all his words. "Okay?"

"Good." Hayden leans forward and slips a gun into my holster without touching me. "Safety is on. I know you've handled a gun before since you killed your uncle. Have you handled one prior to that?"

"Uh..."

Hayden's head snaps to Parker. "Are you fucking for real?"

Parker spins in his seat to glare at Hayden. "Stop being a little shit. I said I've got his six, that's all that matters. Got it?"

They stare each other down for a few long moments before Jacob leans forward, effectively jostling Hayden out of my line of vision.

"You got it, Parker. The boss just wants us to be safe."

Parker deflates a little and nods, then hops out of the car. He makes his way to the passenger door and opens it for me, lines of his body taut, jaw tight. I hop out and stand in front of him, staring up at him in the pitch-black cover for the mission.

"You don't have to put yourself on the line for me," I whisper.

Parker's eye twitches and he glances over the car at someone. "I do though, you just don't understand why yet."

"Parker..."

He snaps his head back to me. "Just do as I say in there."

"What are we doing *in there*?"

"That's for us to know and you to stay ignorant of," Hayden calls out. "Plausible deniability."

"Not if I kill someone," I argue.

Hayden winks at me as he passes by with serious swagger. "Well, if someone catches on to tonight, Parker will go down for the murder. That's the deal."

My heart catches in my chest. Again? I want to say something, want to... I don't know what I fucking want to do, but I want to do something. But just as I'm working up the courage to utter a word, Parker walks away with a nod of his head toward the building. All of the guys, including my brother, pause in the shadow of the building. I follow close to Parker's back, knowing without being told that he'll guide me through the evening.

"I'm just pissed you get to kill someone before me," Reid mumbles to my left.

I glance over at him with an apologetic grimace. "I think he's only letting me do it because of Uncle Marc."

Reid shrugs. "Still. I only got a taser."

"Because I don't trust you with a gun," Dante retorts from in front of us.

Reid doesn't even argue, which surprises me. He just places his hand on the taser in a holster on his hip. I glance down to the gun safely tucked in the holster against my chest. A queasy feeling threatens to overtake me, but I push it deep down.

"Parker and Dante are going to go in first to clear security," Hayden says when Parker and Dante break formation to head inside.

Five minutes later, the door opens and Dante nods for us to come inside. Parker squats down beside an unconscious security guard. When he unfolds his long body to stand, I can't help but stare. Parker is always beautiful, but he's magnificent in his element. Which happens to be murder. Apparently, murder for pay is his element.

"Yeah, they're all kind of hot when they're working," Reid says with a snort. "I cannot tell you how many times I've made Dante fuck me right after a mission."

I wrinkle my nose in disgust. "Reid, please."

Reid shoots me a look. "Don't worry, Mason, you'll get there too."

"I'm just here to kill someone," I lie, because that's not all this is at all.

Reid snorts again, but this time loud enough to attract the attention of his minder. Dante shoots him a look and lifts a finger to his mouth in the universal sign for shush. But all Reid does is grin real wide, lift his hand, then slowly pretend to wind up his middle finger.

"Sit and spin," Reid mouths before blowing Dante a kiss.

Dante basically seethes but goes back to tying the security guard's hands.

"You antagonize him a lot," I point out.

Reid winks. "He likes it."

"If you have time to chat, you have time to help," Hayden says as he walks by us.

Reid rolls his eyes but gestures for us to follow behind Hayden. The other boys fall in behind us as Hayden leads us down the dark hallway. Emergency lights come on as we walk, and the quiet hush of the deserted warehouse makes me vaguely uncomfortable. The place looks empty; there's no one here for me to kill.

"There are two more security guards before we reach the guy you get the honor of executing," Hayden says to me over his shoulder. "Orders are to leave guards alive because they're hired, not aware of what Mr. Hall is getting up to."

"What is Mr. Hall guilty of?" I ask.

Hayden makes an annoyed sound. "I told you, plausible deniability. Plus, you really don't want to know."

Well, okay. We turn a corner to find two tired-looking security guards flanking a steel door. They jump, unprepared for the sight of us, but Parker moves around us to shoot them with the tranquilizer gun. Reid's right. It *is* fucking sexy watching him work. Parker shakes his head to clear his vision of the wisps of hair that have escaped the bun on the back of his head. Dante and Parker break from us to tie the security guards' arms behind their backs as they lie zonked out on the floor.

"How long do those work for?" I ask, full of curiosity.

"Approximately three hours," Jacob replies from behind me. "Accidentally tested on me first."

"That's why Dante doesn't get the tranq gun," Parker calls out.

Dante's shoulders lift to his ears. "It was an accident."

"Lessons learned." Hayden steps forward, presses a button on the steel doors, and they slide open.

There's a desk ten feet into the room, where a frightened-looking man stands.

"Now listen here. I don't know who you are, but you are barking up the wrong tree."

"Do we look like we give a shit," Hayden says, voice an

octave lower, and angrier. "Hand me the computer, and even if you wiped it, we'll get what's on it."

The man swallows loudly and moves to reach under his desk. "Listen…"

"No, *you* listen. You're dead anyway, and if you press that emergency button, the police will arrive in time to find you killed and disemboweled. So stop moving." Hayden steps forward and holds his gloved hands out, wiggling his fingers when the guy doesn't budge. "I said give me the goddamn laptop, you ugly motherfucker."

The man hands the laptop over with trembling hands.

"Ready?" Parker asks.

I tilt my head to look at him. "I'm not sure. What if he's not a bad guy? What if it's a misunderstanding?"

Hayden snorts. "Do you want to see what's on his laptop? It'll make you hurl up your intestines."

Well. That'll have to be good enough. Parker urges me on with a nod, so I take a step forward, and the guy looks at me in profound disbelief.

"This twink is gonna kill me? I mean, seriously, I deserve at least that one over there to kill me," he says, nodding toward Dante.

"I'm not a twink. I'm almost six feet," I argue pitifully.

I look back at Dante to find him pointing at himself, then glancing around. "Trust me, you *really* want him to kill you instead of me. I use my hands when I kill someone."

Reid stares up at Dante with stars in his eyes.

I don't think I'm made for this.

"Take the gun out," Parker says quietly, voice level and making a shiver work its way through me. "Yeah, that's it. Now turn off the safety, the button on the left. Good job."

Everything calms under Parker's gentle direction. My

mouth is dry and my fingers sweat in the leather gloves as I lift the gun to point it at the man's chest. He still looks like he thinks this is an elaborate prank, which oddly makes me feel more resolute that I need to do this. Not only to prove it to the guys, but to this despicable asshole who questions my ability to kill him just by my looks alone.

"Now," Parker whispers against my ear, sending a rush of heat through me. "Pull the trigger. There's going to be blood, but at this position, most of it should scatter backwards. When he falls to the ground, you'll step around the desk and aim another shot at his head while he watches. You're his killer, show him."

And without a second thought, I pull the trigger, and the guy falls behind the desk just like Parker predicted. I turn my head to grin at Parker, heart racing in excitement instead of anxiety.

"I did it!" I whisper-shout.

Parker's grin illuminates the dark room. "Yeah, now you get to finish it. Go on."

I step around the desk, with Parker's warmth close at my back. The guy stares up at me, clutching his chest, wiggling as if squirming like a maggot on the ground can save him from his certain destiny. There is an odd thrill to killing him, knowing he's done such despicable things, they won't even sully me with the knowledge. And it's an anxiety-riddled six-foot twink who's going to end his life.

I aim the gun at his head and pull the trigger without a second thought. Some blood sprays up, so I urgently step back, bumping into Parker. His hand comes out to steady my elbow and my body lights up from that one touch. Oh. Parker pulls away like he's burned me, a flush on his high cheekbones.

"Sorry, it was instinctual, I'm so sorry—"

"It's okay," I say, interrupting him, because it was okay. It's fine.

Suddenly, Hayden appears beside me wearing a totally perplexed expression. He shoots me an inquisitive look before turning his gaze back to the man bleeding out on the ground.

"Huh," Hayden says in obvious disbelief. "I didn't think you'd actually do it."

"You owe me fifty dollars," Jacob teases while dropping to the ground. He presses a gloved finger to the man's bloody neck, then looks up at me with a grin so similar to Parker's that I feel a little thrown. Twins. "I knew you had it in you."

I can still feel the warmth of Parker's hand as it rested briefly on my arm to steady me. My heart pounds in my chest, but not from anxiety, from the thrill of finally doing something without thinking about it fifty million ways to Sunday.

Jacob stands and nods toward the laptop Hayden is clutching to his chest. "Do you need to delete camera footage of us being here?"

Hayden rolls his eyes deeply. "I disabled the cameras. Why do you think there aren't any cops here yet?"

Jacob's eye twitches in the corner but he remains silent. I return my gaze to Parker to find him already watching me, that same calm, understanding smile on his lips from the last time he watched me kill a man. A sense of knowing washes over me. Deep understanding that maybe, in some way, I was always supposed to end up *right* here. It's such an intense feeling I feel a little dizzy with the knowledge. I must sway on my feet because Parker takes a hesitant step closer, like he'll grab me if he must, but he prefers not to in order to protect my space.

"I'm going to get a complex about not being allowed to kill anyone," Reid whines, breaking whatever spell Parker and I are under.

I clear my throat and look away, toward Reid at the back of the room. "I think it's the right call to not let you kill anyone."

Dante looks absolutely thrilled, but Reid's fury is quick and violent. Just as he's about to say something, Dante covers his mouth with a big hand and tugs my brother back against his chest. Whatever Dante dips down to whisper in Reid's ear settles him, but his eyes stay squinted and his chest heaves a little.

"Let's go," Hayden orders, and like that, everyone moves.

The emergency lights in the warehouse flicker on in front of us, then turn off as we exit the building still under the cover of night. We all walk fast back to the car. Once we're all in the safety of the vehicle, the silence is a little overwhelming. Parker fiddles with the stereo and puts on the same singer as earlier, which seems to appease everyone in the back seat.

When we get back to their house, everyone hops out of the car in a hurry, except for Hayden.

He leans forward on the console, careful not to touch me, and eyes me with the same look someone might give a zombie. Finally, he sighs from deep in his chest and nods in approval at Parker.

"Welcome to the team, Red."

"Oh..." I don't know what to say.

Hayden turns to fix Parker with a softer—but similar— look. "You're still liable for him until Robin gives the go-ahead to make him official. Just like Dante was liable for Reid. Hopefully this one doesn't get kidnapped and almost blow our cover."

Hayden hops out of the car before Parker can even form a reply.

"Is he always like that?"

Parker's eyebrows furrow. "An asshole?"

"No. Bossy?"

"Well," Parker says slowly as he starts the drive back home, "he is the boss."

"I thought Jacob was the boss?"

Parker's howl of laughter is so genuine and raw that I can't help but grin. Maybe it's worth saying something wrong if it makes him laugh like that. I get the feeling Parker doesn't laugh as much as he could or should. He's got the sort of face made for smiling, especially when those dimples pop in his cheeks. Devastating—that's what Parker has the ability to be to me.

"Jacob is definitely not the boss, but he wishes he was, so maybe that's why he treats Hayden the way he does."

"How does he treat Hayden?"

Parker looks thoughtful for a moment. "Like he's waiting for Hayden to fail."

Interesting. We spend the rest of the car ride in comfortable silence. The weight of the night finally hits me, and so does the exhaustion that comes with it. I killed a man tonight. A second man in the span of a week is dead at my hands. And I can't explain why it gives me no anxiety. Maybe I *am* broken, but not in the way I always expected.

But god do I need a shower. I want to scrub my skin raw, climb into bed, and sleep for an eternity in my nice, clean bed. We undress quickly in the garage, until we're left in just boxer briefs, but I pointedly aim my curious gaze away from Parker to avoid getting caught staring at him with drool dripping down my chin. I carefully peel the clothing off me, folding it. I'm sure it'll need dry cleaning at some specialty murderer dry cleaner.

Parker's quiet and subdued, but still the comforting presence my humming nerves seem to need. I stare down at our shoes side by side, the custom-made murder shoes.

"You custom ordered murder shoes for me," I whisper, feeling out of body after the events of the evening.

Parker chuckles darkly. "I guess I did."

I turn my head to gaze up at him. "Do you want to kiss me?"

A bittersweet smile lifts Parker's lips. "Yeah, I think I do."

"You're straight," I point out, heart pounding in my chest.

"Maybe not as much as I thought because it's never hurt me so badly before at the idea of going my entire life not touching someone."

Oh god. That's simultaneously the sweetest and saddest thing anyone has ever said to me.

"I want to kiss you too," I admit, a rock stuck in my throat.

Parker's eyes darken in the heavy night that surrounds us. I've never felt this level of attraction for someone before. Half of it is Parker's looks, how beautiful he is, how attractive I find him, but the other half is because of how careful he is with me. He's not careful out of fear, but careful out of *respect* for me, which makes all the difference in the world.

"Not tonight though."

Parker grins. "Of course."

"But maybe you can sleep in my bed with me?"

"That sounds great, Mace."

"And keep calling me that. I really like it." I can feel the flush working its way across my cheeks and down my neck. Parker's eyes only seem to darken more at my admission.

"You better take your shower before I do something neither of us is ready for. I'll meet you in your room."

The clear order in his tone has my feet moving before my brain can catch up. He follows me up the stairs, but we go to our separate rooms. I stand still in the bathroom for a moment, reorienting myself to my new reality. I turn the water up as high as I can take it until the room is filled with steam and my skin is dewy from the humidity. Gritting my teeth, I stand under the scalding hot stream of water for a few seconds to acclimate myself to my new reality. Finally I shake myself free. It takes me fifteen minutes to scrub my body pink with my antibacterial bodywash.

Once I've dried off, done my evening absolutions, and dressed in a pair of sweatpants and an old T-shirt, I open the bathroom door to find Parker lounging on my bed. My body goes cold and hot at the same time, emotions warring inside me. I feel like Parker belongs there, but he also terrifies me. What if I can't give him everything he needs and he casts me aside? *I am loved and worthy of love*, I remind myself, surely making my therapist proud if she knew.

I slowly join Parker on the bed, lying on my side to face him. We're two closed parentheses, our hands between us, not touching, but almost. And if I had courage, and if I wasn't so afraid of everything, I'd close the scant space between us to touch my pinkie finger to his own. But I don't. Instead, we lie there staring at each other in the muted darkness of my bedroom.

Parker slowly lifts his hand from between us to dance it over my face in the mimicry of a touch. If I close my eyes, I can imagine the pressure, soft and kind, like he's gentling a wary, unbroken horse.

"I want to touch you one day, like this," Parker murmurs, voice full of desire. "Your skin against mine will be the closest I'll ever get to God."

"Parker..."

"Sorry, I just..." Parker makes this confused, worried sort of face that I find way more handsome than I should. "I wonder what you taste like."

"Probably toothpaste. I brush my teeth, like, five times a day."

"Mint, but behind that, I bet you taste sweet. Like a Shirley Temple."

I close my eyes tight and dip my head to avoid his gaze. Parker rests his hand back between us, seemingly catching on to my sudden shyness. He's too much. He's going to kill me before I even get the chance to try kissing him.

"Is me on the bed too much for you?" Parker asks.

"No, I don't think so."

"Good," Parker says gruffly. "We should try to sleep."

I get under the covers with a contented sigh and snuggle into the familiar comfort of my bed. Parker's gentle breathing lulls me to sleep without a worry for the murder I committed earlier this evening.

CHAPTER 8

PARKER

As I sit in class, I think back to this morning. Mason was sound asleep beside me when I was finally roused from my own deep sleep. His dark red hair hung in messy waves across his face, his lips plump as the pillow pushed his cheek up and out. It'd taken everything inside me to not reach out and touch, to not take something from him in his sleep that would be a violation. But I respected Mason too much to even attempt it.

Halfway through class I'm yawning and wishing I'd stopped to grab a cup of coffee. Once class wraps up, I rush out and head toward the campus coffee joint. A whistle in the air stops me in my tracks, and I wait for Jacob to catch up to me.

"Sup?" Jacob asks as he jostles me to the edge of the sidewalk.

"Just finished class, you know, as is required to maintain our scholarships."

Jacob rolls his eyes so hard it looks painful. "I also attend class. You and Hayden need a new schtick."

"Don't lump me in with Hayden."

"Ughhhhh." Jacob pushes me again, this time making me stumble into the grass that still hasn't yet recovered from the bite of winter. I freeze and glare at him until he rolls his eyes again. "Fine. Sorry. Listen, Reid was serious about Dante's birthday party. We're having a game night tonight."

I really do not want to go to this party. Perhaps I'll make something up. Sometimes when I want to be left alone, I tell Jacob I have a separate mission, assuming he won't mention it to Hayden because Hayden is the one who gives me the missions. This sounds like a perfect time to do that. My next mission isn't for a few more days, but he doesn't need to know that.

"All right, but I'll have to leave early because I have a separate mission."

"Always a separate mission," Jacob grumbles under his breath.

"Do you have a problem?"

"No."

Jacob follows me into the coffee shop like a lost puppy. I order us both Americanos from the sweet barista behind the counter. With a smile and grin, I join Jacob where he stands scrolling through his phone at the pickup counter.

"I get the vibe Dante doesn't enjoy surprises, so I don't think this is going to go over real well."

Jacob snorts in agreement. "You and I both." He pockets his phone and stares hard at the menu. "I oddly think Reid is good for him though. Those two have some toxic codependency thing going on, but Dante is definitely less angry than he used to be."

I grunt but don't deign him with an answer. I don't like to gossip about Dante. We're... friends? So I try to keep things he tells me in confidence even from my own brother. Just like I respect Jacob's privacy. I'm a steel trap but I'm also Switzerland. No information goes in or out and no side is ever taken.

"Reid doesn't know when *our* birthday is, right?"

Jacob looks anywhere but at me. Oh hell no.

"Jacob."

Jacob grimaces and rushes forward to grab our two drinks. I grab mine from him with a deep frown, patiently waiting for him to explain himself to me.

"Listen... Hayden knows when our birthday is, and he told Reid."

What the hell? "Why does Hayden know?"

I'm met with silence and the sight of Jacob's back as he flees the coffee shop. Now I'm getting irritated.

"Fuck you, Jacob Chambers! Why does Hayden know our birthday?"

I hustle after Jacob because I'm going to get the truth out of him no matter what. Finally, he stops close to the quad, where we're out of earshot from the small number of afternoon stragglers between classes.

"Hayden made me tell him. He wanted to know everyone's birthdays."

I blink slowly. "Okay... but why does Reid know."

Jacob makes a noise somewhere between a grunt in disbelief and a snort of annoyance. "Are you serious right now? They're, like, best friends. You do not pay attention."

"Hayden and Reid are best friends?" I ask in confusion. I don't see it. They're both opposites and bossy and so blond... Well, Reid is less blond now that he's dyeing his hair silver and blue. But he's blond in spirit, so it counts.

"Yes," Jacob says with an air of regret.

"Well, whatever, but we don't need birthday parties."

"I don't know why you hate our birthday so much."

"Because we'll have to share it for the rest of our lives, and we've shared everything else, so I like to pretend it's just another day."

"Parker." Jacob says my name like I've personally offended him.

"I'll see you tonight."

Jacob calls my name when I'm almost out of hearing range. Turning around, I find him grinning and saluting me, probably in agreement of keeping his mouth shut. Whatever.

The house is quiet when I finally arrive home in the late afternoon. I don't know what Mason does now that he's not working for his uncle. Maybe I should ask him. I hang my jacket up and put my bag in the living room so I can hopefully remember to do my homework tomorrow.

Mason's sitting at his computer watching a video when I pause outside his study door. He looks very serious, his lips drawn down in a frown, eyebrows furrowed in concentration.

I knock on the door to gain his attention. "Hey."

Mason looks like he's been slapped. He flushes to the roots of his hair and slams his laptop shut. That's interesting. I squint and look at him more closely, noticing the red splotches on his pale cheeks, the tension in his shoulders as he slumps over to avoid my gaze.

"Do you want me to ask or do you want me to leave you alone about it?"

Mason blinks up at me in confusion. "Seriously?"

I shrug. "I only ever want to know what you *want* me to know."

Mason makes a startled, disbelieving sort of laugh, then furiously shakes his head. "You're a literal dream. Do you know that?"

"Uh…"

"You're just sort of perfect… for me," Mason says sourly, as if irritated by it.

"Sorry?"

"Anyway…" Mason squares his shoulders and stares me down. "I was looking at porn."

"Oh. Was it good?"

He saws his hand back and forth. "Porn hasn't ever really done anything for me. I get kind of caught up in it. I wonder if they're really enjoying it, if they're happy, if they smell funny. Like, what if one of their breaths just reeks but the other doesn't say anything and kisses them just for the sake of the porno." Mason gasps. "What if one of them has mono!?"

I lean against the door with a smile. "I guess that's possible."

Mason huffs and gets this cute concerned look on his face. "Plus, I'm not that interested in anal."

"I don't think everyone is."

"Have you ever done it?" Mason asks so seriously that it makes me snort a laugh. I guess we're having this conversation, then. Right before we go over to the house for Dante's birthday party.

"Have I had anal sex?"

Mason blinks, his mouth turning down. "Actually, *don't* tell me, because then I'll just wonder if you're constantly thinking about how much you miss it."

All right, that's it. He's going to work himself into a tizzy. I stride across the room, watching as his face goes a little soft at my proximity. Dropping to my knees in front of him, I stay out of reach since he's not ready for me to touch him yet. I'm not sure I am either, because I can already tell one touch won't be even close to enough. Not with Mason. Never.

"I can promise you with absolute certainty that I won't be thinking about anyone but you when we're together. In whatever form of intimacy is allowed between us."

Mason groans and covers his face. "See"—Mason peeks at me from between his fingers, words mumbled—"when you say shit like that, I really want to kiss you."

My grin is borderline painful, which just makes Mason groan in frustration again. I stand back up and look down at him, trying to make myself have a considering sort of look, instead of all-out appreciative.

"Tonight is Dante's birthday party. You'll come with me."

"Right," Mason agrees, throat clicking on a loud swallow. "What are you wearing?"

"My usual."

"Slacks and a dress shirt with the sleeves rolled up to your elbows to make everyone drool over your epic forearms?"

I snort. "Epic forearms?"

Mason sighs dreamily. "You've no idea."

Huh. I look down at my forearms but don't notice anything epic about them. Shrugging, I hook my thumb over my shoulder to point toward the kitchen.

"I'm going to go make myself a small snack. Want anything?"

Mason waves his hand dismissively but follows me into the kitchen regardless. I end up making him a cup of tea, and he smiles gratefully at me over the rim. After a small snack of a green apple with some nut butter, I send Mason upstairs to get ready for the evening. When he asks what to wear, I just shrug and let him decide what he thinks will make me happy. But truly, he could wear a burlap sack, and I'd find him the most beautiful being in any room.

I stand downstairs in the foyer as the sun is setting, casting the living room in early evening darkness. Mason descends the stairs wearing a pair of navy dress slacks and a button-down white dress shirt that hugs his slim form. He sends me a shy smile that does more for me than the outfit ever could.

"How old is Dante anyway?" Mason asks as he follows me into the garage.

I open the door and wait for him to get all buckled in. "Twenty-two."

"He's the eldest?"

I hum agreement, then close the door. The car is a little cold, so I turn the heat up as I back out of the driveway. Mason cutely snuggles back into the leather seat while tucking his hands under his thighs.

"I assume you don't want anyone knowing... about... whatever this is?" I ask quietly.

Mason shoots me a severe look. "Absolutely not. It would be embarrassing for them to all find out and then in a week or two for you to realize... Well. Let's just keep it to ourselves for a little while."

I fight against the urge to argue with him. I know what I'm signing up for with Mason. His anxiety and quirks don't bother me at all. In fact, in a way I can't explain, they intrigue me, making it feel like everything he shows me is earned out of explicit trust.

All the lights for the house are lit up when I park in the driveway. Balloons hang from the brick ballasts out front. Reid really went all out. The house is warm and inviting when we step inside. Laughter rings out from the backyard, so I nod that direction in order for Mason to follow. When I slide the glass door open, everyone turns toward us. Mason waves shyly from behind me. Dante's lips quirk into a knowing, wry twist of lips even as Reid sits in his lap.

Twinkling lights hang from the porch railing and from the two sparse winter-dead trees in the backyard. A table of appetizers sits to the right, and there's a steel bucket full of icy beer. I dip down to grab one, then join the rest of them in one of the Adirondack chairs that get way more play in the summer. Reid's even gotten a gas fire pit going in the middle of the circle between us.

Mason stands awkwardly behind me for a few seconds before mumbling something that sounds a lot like *oh hell whatever*, then sits on the railing of the chair since all the other chairs are occupied. I shift a little to the left to give him more room so that I don't actually touch him. Mason must notice because he looks down at me with this soft and fond sort of look that makes me wish so desperately I could touch him on purpose in front of everyone. So that they all know he's mine.

"Happy birthday, big guy," I say while tipping my beer at Dante.

Dante grins, but it's a genuine smile, not that scary fake one that unsettles us all. "It's actually tomorrow."

Everyone stills. Reid turns slowly to look down at Dante. "You said it was the last day of February. That's today... the twenty-eighth."

Dante clears his throat awkwardly. "Not always."

Huh? Silence fills the void for a few moments before Hayden cackles. "His real birthday is *leap day*, you idiots."

Reid's eyes go big, then a terrifying smirk works its way across his face.

"Oh no," Mason mumbles in fear.

"So you're technically only five years old."

Dante narrows his eyes in warning. "No, Reid. I'm twenty-two."

"But your birthday doesn't actually exist," Reid argues, voice tinged with glee.

"Reid."

"Oh my god, were you on the news? Sometimes those cute little leap day babies are on the news because they're *so* special."

"I was not on the news as a newborn," Dante deadpans.

Just as Reid clearly is about to press further and ask another question, Dante covers Reid's mouth with his large palm. Reid's nose wrinkles and his eyebrows furrow, but he goes still when Dante whispers something in his ear. A moment later, Dante removes his hand, and Reid clears his throat.

"I hope everyone brought presents," Reid says softly.

I grimace and look toward Jacob, who only rolls his eyes and nods toward the table by the front door. Oh, thank god. The doorbell rings, which has all of us craning our heads to look toward the door in fear.

"Oh, calm down, it's just pizza delivery." Reid waves his hands in frustration while passing by us all to head inside. He stops by the sliding door to cast a look back at Mason. "Help me, please."

Mason sends me an unsure smile but dutifully follows his little brother inside. I watch him go, because it's an amazing view, then turn back to the guys to take a sip of my beer. The beer is cool and crisp, and I almost spit it out when Hayden fixes me with a stern look and asks, "Are you fucking him?"

"No," I reply firmly.

Hayden has the gall to look disbelieving. "Hmm."

"And if I was, would it matter?"

"No, but it might cause you to make bad decisions," Hayden finally says.

"I disagree. I think what I feel for Mason will force me to make better decisions."

Hayden tilts his head at me like an eagle watching prey. "How so?"

I lift my gaze to Jacob and see understanding there as his gaze flits over to Hayden. Oh. That's when it all clicks. How could I not see it all this time? Jacob's gaze goes distant as he tears his eyes away from Hayden to look inside over my shoulder.

"When you care about someone besides yourself, put their safety above your own, the decisions you make are for *everyone* instead of just yourself."

Hayden snorts in disbelief. "Whatever. None of you would die for me out there, of that I'm sure."

"I would," I say loudly, pulling his attention back to me. "I'd die for you, boss."

"Me too," Dante chimes in.

Hayden rolls his eyes. "Sure."

"Hayden," Jacob says gruffly, but Hayden just ignores him. I watch as Hayden crosses his arms over his broad chest and tosses himself back in the chair as if attempting to make himself invisible.

Reid breaks the spell by sauntering in with plates full of pizza. He and Mason take turns handing them out before Mason sits back down on the edge of my chair. I set the half-empty beer bottle on the other side of the chair and grab my pizza. We all chat quietly as we eat, most of us teasing or roasting one another, notably Dante, which he takes good-naturedly because that's the kind of guy he is.

I sneak glances at Mason every time he laughs at something stupid one of us says. He eats half of a slice of pizza before placing the plate on the ground and carefully wiping his fingers on a napkin. When he catches me staring, he thinks it's out of want of a napkin, so he hands me one, and I take it to avoid letting my eyes tell him the truth of my stare.

"Presents!" Reid announces, excitedly slapping his hands together.

I say a silent prayer that Jacob got Dante something good as Reid hands over gift bags and a single box. Hayden still looks sulky, but he perks up a little when Dante decides to open the glittery purple bag first. Must be from him.

Dante's eyes go misty when he opens the bag, then he looks at Hayden with unrestrained joy. "Really?"

Hayden waves Dante's emotional question away. "It's just one time."

"What is it?" I ask because I'm nosy.

"It's a voucher to help with hacking on any mission of my choosing."

We're all silent because that is a huge deal. Dante is never allowed to help with hacking. Hayden must feel very giving today. Mason shifts uncomfortably on the edge of the chair. It takes everything inside me not to wrap my arm around him, tug him onto my lap, and bury my face in the crook of his neck.

"There's more presents." Hayden points at the other gift bags. "Keep going."

Dante opens up the present from me and Jacob, which contains gift cards for custom Chucks. The final gift bag is from Reid, if evidenced by the way Dante's eyes go large and he whispers something to Reid that is thankfully not for our ears. Finally, he grabs the box from the ground with a curious sort of look.

"Who's this from?" Dante asks with a frown.

Reid looks around at all of us in confusion. "I assumed one of you?"

All of us shake our heads and shrug. Dante doesn't seem bothered by it as he digs into the wrapping paper. He opens the box, and after a second of rustling the tissue paper inside, he pulls out a frame. A terrifying growl escapes him as he shoves the framed picture at Reid. The look on Reid's face isn't that dissimilar from Dante, except Reid's lips are pursed in disgust.

"Well." Reid looks at us all, then turns the picture around with a flourish. "That's unexpected, huh?"

It's a framed photo of The Carver, who Dante had briefly thought he killed after Reid's kidnapping, until Robin bore news of his escape. The picture is a selfie in front of the house, and the guy is wearing the biggest shit-eating grin I've ever seen in my life, all while sipping at a whipped cream–laden iced coffee.

"You gotta admit, he has flair," Jacob notes with a hint of hero worship.

"He tried to kill Reid," Dante reminds everyone with a deep growl.

"Well, that's not entirely true," Reid argues.

Dante shifts his confused gaze to Reid. "What?"

"Uh... he just tortured me. He wasn't aiming to kill."

"You needed a blood transfusion," Mason points out, voice high pitched and a little hysterical.

"Yeah, but, like, I didn't die."

"Oh my god, he has Stockholm syndrome," Jacob says on a theatrical gasp.

"Whatever." Reid rolls his eyes and tosses the signed

picture over his head so that it lands in the backyard. Amazing. "I'm sure it's just... a little joke. Haha?"

Dante growls from deep in his chest and stares listlessly into the backyard. Birthday ruined, I guess. I help Mason and Reid clean up outside as Jacob tries to talk Dante down from whatever ledge he's on. Once the party is all cleaned up and the beers have been put away, we move to the living room to hang out since the air is getting a little too chilly outside despite the new fire pit.

Hayden turns the television on so we can play some video games. It starts up on a news channel, and Jacob holds his hand out for Hayden to pause.

"Wait," Jacob orders, voice firm enough to catch my attention.

Hayden moves to stand beside him, effectively blocking the television. "Holy shit."

"You guys either need to share what's happening or sit down so we can see for ourselves," Reid shouts.

Hayden and Jacob both immediately sit to give us a view of the screen. The news broadcast says in block letters *BOTH DEAD SENATORS GUILTY OF PARTICIPATING IN A SEX TRAFFICKING RING.*

"Oh my god," Mason exclaims on a pained-sounding gasp.

Hayden quickly whips his head around. "Did you know?"

Mason's eyes widen with fear. "I had no idea! I mean, I killed him because he deserved it, but I didn't know... that he..." The words seem to get caught in his throat. He looks to me in need, and the only thing I can think to do is smile warmly at him, hoping to settle whatever nerves are starting to roil in his gut.

"Let's go home," I say quietly, shocked that his house is starting to feel more like home to me.

Mason visibly slumps in relief. "Okay."

"You're leaving? Now?" Hayden asks accusingly.

"Yes. We'll talk this over if it develops into anything."

Hayden eyes me shrewdly but remains uncharacteristically quiet. After shaking hands with Dante and wishing him happy birthday, Mason and I take our leave. The night air is cooler and crisper, so I hurry him to the car with my hand hovering over the small of his back. If I close my eyes, I can almost pretend he can feel my phantom touch.

Once we get back home, we go about our separate night-time routines as usual. But like the other night, I join him on the bed after my thorough shower. Mason's hair is slightly damp and there are dark smudges under his eyes. Lifting my hand, I trace the air around his jaw, cheeks, and his lips. Red blooms across his cheeks. I pretend the flush is from desire, from need for me. It stirs the deep need inside me to have him, but also to protect him in a way I can't explain. Even from myself if necessary.

"Soon," Mason whispers so that I can feel the damp puff of air against the pads of my fingers.

"However long, including never," I promise him.

Mason closes his eyes with a content sigh. Moments later, he's sound asleep, and I watch him for a little while before sleep claims me for her own.

CHAPTER 9

MASON

P arker has slept beside me every single night for the past
five days. Except for tonight, because he has a very
important mission. He'd left in his hot-as-hell mission
clothes, including his murder shoes, and he'd given me his
gentle smile that is starting to make me sweat instead of
calming me down. Now it's a little past midnight and I can't
sleep.

The bed doesn't feel right without the gentle dip on his
side from his overly warm body. I mean, is his temperature
always a million degrees? Not that I hate it because most
nights I'm cold. The warmth of his body lulls me to sleep.
Without him my body aches from the cold pressing in on me.
What will happen when we finally touch? Will I ignite into
flames from all this wanting?

After tossing and turning for a while, I finally decided to
just give up. I can't go downstairs because Parker's whole *you
can't be downstairs without me* order is still in effect even when
he's not home.

Around one in the morning, the sound of the car pulling

into the garage has me rolling out of bed in excitement. The garage door creaks open when I'm halfway down the stairs. For a second, fear shoots through me, as I worry that it's not Parker, that it's the same people who stole Reid. I sink down to a crouch on the stairs, watching fearfully as Parker walks into the shadowed hallway. He's clutching his side, breathing strangely, and walking with a limp. Fuck.

"Parker?" I call out softly.

Parker startles a little but then finds me crouching down on the stairs. Under his gaze, I stand to my full height, only now realizing I'm just wearing boxer briefs and one of Parker's larger T-shirts. His nostrils flare at the sight of me and my cock takes immediate notice. Oh.

"Why aren't you asleep?" Parker asks, sounding oddly out of breath.

"You weren't there and it felt wrong. I couldn't sleep."

Parker swears under his breath, then lifts the hand not clutching his ribs to tiredly rub his face. He looks so exhausted. My heart aches for him, stirring up this urge to take care of him like he so often takes care of me.

"Come on," I say, holding my hand out to him in invitation.

He looks at my hand and firms his jaw. "Go on. Let me shower and then I'll join you on the bed. Give me a bit?"

"No."

Parker's eyebrows wing up in clear surprise. "No?"

"I want to see why you're clutching your side like that."

Parker huffs a frustrated laugh. "Go on. I'll see you in a minute."

I wiggle my fingers at him once more. "Come on. You can use my shower, it's bigger."

Parker swallows loudly but gives up his fight. It takes him

double the time it normally does to climb the stairs. I move aside so he can limp into the bathroom under the soft lighting. He glances at me over his shoulder and sighs deeply at whatever look he sees on my face.

"I'm fine," Parker grumbles, clearly annoyed.

"I'll decide on that." I take a step forward, so our bare feet almost touch. "Take your clothes off."

"Mason."

"Parker."

He stares at me. I stare at him.

Finally, he gives up and starts to unbutton his shirt one-handed. I dip down under the sink and grab a pair of latex gloves. Parker's eyebrows furrow in a very cute manner, but I try to not show him that I find him adorable by keeping my face as blank as possible.

"Uh."

I wave his concern away while snapping on the gloves. "We're not playing doctor. Unless you're interested in that?"

Parker looks simultaneously turned on and a little confused. "I don't know. Maybe I am."

I huff out a delighted laugh. Batting hands away so he can go back to clutching his side, I slowly unbutton his shirt, tenderly easing it over his broad shoulders. Parker hisses as I get the shirt over the shoulder on the side that's causing him pain. I ignore whatever injury he has to move on to unbuckling his belt. The temperature in the room goes up about ten million degrees as I carefully tug his belt off. I can hear every quiet inhale and exhale from Parker, even feel his warm, sweet breath on my face. It doesn't gross me out like I once thought it would.

Once I've got his pants unbuttoned, I wiggle them down over his hips, his strong thighs, then let them fall to the ground. Finally, Parker stands only in his boxer briefs. Ignoring the beauty of the specimen in front of me is hard, but I decide to focus on his injury. With a loud, displeased sigh, Parker lets his hand drop from his right side. His ribs have already turned a dark purple, and I can't help but reach out to gently touch the blossoming bruise. Parker releases an agonized hiss and I go to pull away, but he stops me with a firm shake of his head.

"Wasn't... Wasn't the pain. It was the fact you touched me."

I lift my gaze to his, catching the hot desire in his eyes. "Oh."

I look back to his ribs, then let my gaze drift down to his hardening cock in his boxer briefs. "I've barely touched you and you're hard..." I wonder aloud.

Parker chuckles ruefully. "Mace, I get hard if I'm just in the same room as you."

I swallow loudly. "Because of me?"

"Yeah," Parker says gruffly. "Only because of you."

"Can you... Can you shower with that injury? Brush your teeth?"

Parker tilts his head, and his grin is slow and lecherous. Every bone in my body melts into a puddle of goo just from that one look. Without argument, Parker uses his uninjured arm to push down his underwear, and I try to keep my cool when his erect cock bounces against his stomach. A bead of pre-cum shines against his skin in the muted light of the bathroom. He slowly reaches into the shower with his good arm, and turns it on, the water splashing against the dark tiles the only sound in the room for a few moments. Parker carefully climbs into the shower while maintaining my gaze.

"Are you hard?" Parker asks as he carefully works shampoo into his hair.

"Yeah," I admit, not an ounce embarrassed.

Parker leans against the tiled shower wall, gloriously naked and body on show just for me. Soap trails over his sleek muscles, dripping between his legs, and that's where my attention gets caught. His cock is hard, curving toward his stomach, and easily an inch or two longer than mine and way more girthy. What would it be like to take him into my mouth? Two feelings war in me at once—anxiety prickles into my awareness at the idea of having his cock in my mouth, but the other half of me is aroused in a way I've never been before. How in the world are we going to make this work?

Instead of getting caught up in the anxiety of how it won't work, I let myself get caught up in the tide when Parker starts to work a soapy hand over his cock. Oh Jesus H. Christ. My mouth goes dry and my eyes flick up to meet his fathomless gaze.

"It's okay to want me, Mason."

I grimace but hold his gaze. "What if you change your mind..."

"I never want to hear you say that again," Parker orders, his tone moving through me to shake me to my core. "If I could drop to my knees right now and suck your cock, I would. But I'll settle for just one kiss, even if I have to drink a gallon of Listerine."

"That's the most romantic thing anyone has ever and will ever say to me," I admit through gasping pants. I've never been so turned on in my life. I feel warm and cold at the same time, every single nerve in my body alight at the idea of letting myself touch Parker, and being touched in return.

Parker grins like a hungry wolf. "I think I can do better."

I watch in silence as he sensually washes his entire body, skipping his fingers along the lines of water dripping down his inviting skin. Parker dry is a beautiful sight, but wet is a whole other thing entirely. I think Parker is sexy in any form he takes, but he wants me? The gangly guy that's got curly red hair that grew back that way after chemo as a kid. The guy that doesn't always want to touch or be touched. I feel the anxiety start to swell again, my thoughts start to take on a dark edge, so I focus back on Parker, gaze sharp and wanting, because Parker wants me, however I am. I at least know that.

Parker rinses his hair, then his body, and grabs a clean towel. I'd replaced the one that was in there after my evening shower. Every movement of his body is like that of a cheetah, sleek and practiced. When he works his way toward me at the bathroom counter, I have to grip the granite to keep from falling over in a heap of messy want.

"Do you have mouthwash?" Parker asks so softly that I almost don't hear him.

"Yeah... Yes. I mean, yes, I do." I shift down to grab the bottle from under the counter along with a small paper cup.

Parker grins at me around his toothbrush as he starts to scrub not just at his teeth, but his gums and his tongue. Fuck. Do I have a toothbrushing kink or is it just Parker? After a few minutes, he leans over with a pained groan to spit the foamy toothpaste into the sink. He runs water, splashing with his other hand until all the evidence of toothbrushing is gone. I pour him some Listerine into the paper cup and hold it out to him with shaky fingers.

As he swishes the mouthwash, I replace it under the sink and stand to meet his gaze in the mirror. The damp heat of the bathroom is suddenly replaced with sexual tension thick enough for me to choke on it. Parker winks at me in the mirror, then carefully dips again to spit out the mouthwash. I catch sight of the bruised ribs again, wondering if he needs a hospital, but I'm too caught up in wanting him to do anything about it.

"I'll go see Mandy in the morning," Parker swears.

"You promise?"

"Yeah." Parker nods toward the bedroom. "Are we just going to sleep or...?"

Suddenly, I have to kiss him. I lurch forward to press my lips to his and he lets out a happy but surprised noise. Wrapping my palms around his neck, I tangle my fingers in his soft hair that falls almost to his shoulders. But I notice he isn't touching me or moving his lips.

"Is it bad?" I mumble against his mouth.

"No," Parker says, voice delightfully wrecked. "I just don't want to make a mistake. I don't want to push a line you don't know you have and ruin this and we never get to try again."

Oh. I smile up at him and swipe my thumbs across his tight jaw. "Put your hands on my hips."

Parker momentarily looks like he's going to argue but must think better of it, because a second later his large palms soothingly curve over my hips. A shiver racks me at the touch, sparking a fire inside me that's long since been dead. This time when I kiss him, his lips part under mine, and he coaches me through my first fumbling of a real kiss. He tastes like toothpaste and mouthwash, and my brain deems it acceptable. Nothing about the kiss is gross like I'd feared for so many years. The touch of his tongue against my lips sends a lightning strike of desire down my spine. Oh god.

Parker carefully backs us up toward the bed, and when

my knees hit the mattress, I fall back. He stands over me like some type of god, surveying the bounty laid out before them.

"Can you take your shirt off?" Parker asks with a curious tilt of his head.

I shift up a little and peel my shirt off, leaving me only in my now very tight boxer briefs. Parker smiles down at me in clear satisfaction.

"Can I lie down on top of you? Is that a boundary?"

"I have to be honest with you that we won't know what my lines are until we cross them. But I promise to not go ballistic and say we'll never try again. Even my therapist said..." I trail off, realizing what I just revealed.

"You talked to your therapist about this?"

I blink slowly. "Well, yes. To help me navigate how we can have physical intimacy."

"What did she suggest?"

I wave a hand toward the bathroom. "All that. And also condoms for everything we do in case jizz gives me the ick."

Parker laughs as he stares down at me, then he clutches his side in clear pain. "Can I lie down beside you?"

"Yes. Yes, come on." I wiggle my hands in invitation and smile when he joins me on the bed. He looks so worn out but so very mine. It helps that he smells like my bodywash, adding to those possessive feelings that are sweeping through me.

I roll over onto my side to stare at him and he stares right back. He reaches out his hand to trace the edge of my jaw like he's done all the other nights, but this time he really touches me. I shiver under his touch, not from anxiety but out of the need to have more. One more touch; no, all the touches, now, forever.

"Kiss me again," Parker orders, and when he uses that tone of voice, I can't deny him a thing.

I lean forward to glide my lips over his in a soft kiss. He groans deep in the pit of his belly and moves his hand down to grip my hip so hard I'm sure I'll have bruises tomorrow. I can feel the restraint in his kiss—he's letting me lead, letting me discover what will work for me and what won't. And that's what makes Parker perfect for me. Poison ivy and frost, that's what we are. Anyone else would hurt me, but not Parker, he's just the right amount of everything to leave me alive after this touch. His hands stray from my hips to curve up my back, curling around my shoulders and hold on as we kiss until my lips feel bruised and oversensitive. I never thought it could feel like my mouth belongs to another, but the longer Parker kisses me, the more it feels like my mouth is his to own. My brain shuts off as he trails a line of kisses from my mouth to my cheek, up to my forehead. I let out a sigh and he tugs me closer as if he wishes he could bring me into himself for safekeeping. If Parker could, I think he would.

After pressing another soft kiss to my lips, Parker yawns into the kiss and I pull away with a put-on annoyed look.

"Is my kiss boring?"

Parker smiles with his eyes closed. "Never. Wish I could suck you right now."

"Oh."

"But not tonight. Can we go to sleep?"

"Yes. And tomorrow you'll see Mandy about your ribs?"

"Mhmm." But Parker is already halfway asleep. I pet his arm until he's sound asleep, then watch him for a little while, wondering how I got lucky enough to stumble across this entirely too perfect man. He must have some huge fault I can't look over. Then I almost snort when I remember he's a murderer. *That's a pretty big one there, Mason.* But as I cuddle into the bed, my hand still on his arm, I realize that's not a fault at all, especially since I'm also a murderer now. We can be murderers together.

———

I wake before Parker. Sunlight slashes through the edges of my blackout curtains, highlighting the motes of dust floating in the still morning air. The heat's low since I like it cool, meaning my feet are frozen solid even despite Parker's presence in the bed beside me. Moving carefully so as not to jostle the bed, I roll over onto my side to look at him in the early morning light.

His mouth is slightly open, hair wild and untamed since he went to bed with it wet, and I'm surprised to find it has a little curl to it when it dries naturally. Without his glasses on, his eyelashes don't look as long, but they're still much fuller than mine. A day's worth of stubble lines his defined jaw, and the strange urge to touch him overtakes me. Reaching out, I slowly sweep the pads of my fingers across his jaw. The hair is coarse and prickly, but I don't mind the feel of it. Parker blinks slowly awake at my inquisitive touch.

His curious gaze lands on me, eyebrows furrowing as he realizes the feel of my skin against his is what woke him.

"Did you touch me?" Parker asks, voice still rough from sleep.

"Yeah."

"Mmm." Parker shifts on the bed, tilting his head so he can look at me better. "Thought I dreamt it."

"It's not so bad. My brain knows you showered last night, you've been here all night. I don't know... What germs could you even have?"

"That's true."

"But I likely won't ever kiss you without you brushing your teeth. Sorry, that's a hard line."

Parker's grin would take me to my knees if I was standing. "Duly noted."

"How're your ribs? You promised you'd see Mandy today."

Parker shifts around as if taking stock of his body. I don't miss the wince that he carefully tries to conceal, no doubt in an attempt to get out of seeking medical care.

"They hurt, but I've had worse."

I hum and squint one eye, then the other, which makes Parker smile. I carefully angle my body over his so I can assess the damage. The bruises are even darker now than last night, and there's a decent amount of swelling. I wince internally because, honestly, it looks like he might have a broken rib. Without thinking it through, I dip down really quick and brush a kiss across the worst of the damage. Parker hisses again, like he did last night when I touched him. When I lift up, his eyes are closed tight and his mouth is moving without any sound.

"Parker?"

"I'm reciting the opening lines of *The Canterbury Tales* to stop myself from coming in my boxers. Give me a second."

I sit back on my haunches and cover my mouth with my hand to keep from letting out an entirely inappropriate giggle. Finally, he gets himself under control and opens his eyes to pierce me with a heated look.

"Sorry," I mumble, but I don't mean it for a second.

"Sure."

"Can I go with you? To see Mandy?"

"Eh." Parker groans and tiredly rubs his face. "Then I'll have two of you getting on my case about my injuries."

"Oh, I'm definitely coming now."

Parker smiles like he's enjoying a secret. "Fine."

We do our morning absolutions separately, then I help Parker get dressed in black sweatpants and a loose, soft cashmere sweater that was tucked into the back of my closet. My breath catches in my ribs when I carefully place his glasses on his nose, and he smiles somehow warmly and tiredly at the same time. He's beautiful without his glasses, but with them he looks soft and sweet, which is the Parker that's really starting to work his way into my heart. His face looks pained as we head out into the garage, and I can't take one more second of it.

"I'll drive."

"Nope," Parker says immediately.

"Yes. Give me the keys."

Parker stares at me. I stare at him.

This is becoming a common theme among us, I think. Finally, Parker sighs loudly through his nostrils and tosses me the keys. With a pleased grin, I hold the passenger door open for him, ecstatic at the brief switch in our dynamic. Settling into the driver's seat, I hook my phone up to the stereo and play the *D&D* podcast I listen to in order to settle my nerves.

"What the hell is this?" Parker asks, but his tone is playful.

"A *Dungeons and Dragons* podcast I like."

"Is that a television show? Or a band?"

"Parker." I say his name in utter disgust. "Are you serious?"

He shrugs but the move pains him, so I feel kind of bad

for teasing him. "It's basically a real-life role-playing video game. I've never played, but I like listening to it because it's fun."

"Sounds fun," Parker says with a sigh, tipping his head back against the headrest.

I plug the directions to the diner into the car and navigate us onto the street. The sky is bright blue and the sun is high up in the sky, probably a perfect day to be outside. I try not to glance over at Parker as I drive, but it's hard because my body is so attuned to his presence now. By the time we pull up to the diner, my hands are wrapped so tightly around the steering wheel that I'm afraid I've permanently lost some circulation.

"Hey," Parker says.

I tip my head to look at him. "Yeah?"

"Mandy doesn't have real patients. It'll just be me, you, and her in the clean room at the back of the diner."

"I'm not anxious."

Parker purses his lips as if he doesn't believe me but stays quiet. After hopping out of the car, I jog over to his side to open his door, offering help if he needs it. But I'm learning Parker is strong and resilient, but also stubborn as a mule. He keeps a hand tucked against his side to support himself as he hobbles into the almost empty diner despite it being prime brunch time.

It smells like pancake syrup and slightly burnt coffee, which kind of works together in an odd way. A few old guys sit in the corner chatting over what looks like their third cup of coffee, and the sound of cooking echoes from the kitchen. Mandy swears at the counter and moves toward us, tossing a dishrag over her shoulder.

"You look like you're in pain," Mandy notes with a glance up and down Parker.

"'Cause I am," Parker deadpans.

Mandy tuts and nods toward the back. "Come on, kiddo. I'll set you right."

I follow along behind them with my hands tucked under my armpits to avoid touching anything or anyone. Parker pauses after Mandy enters a sterile-looking medical room and leans against the door so I can walk through without touching a thing. I mouth *thank you* toward him, and he mouths *you're welcome* back, and it feels like this little moment I want to fold up and keep in my pocket forever.

Mandy pats the angled exam chair in the middle of the room. "Hop on."

Parker grimaces but does what she says. "Left ribs."

"And how did that happen?" Mandy asks curiously, one eyebrow raised.

"No comment," Parker says evasively.

"Hmm." Mandy lifts his sweater carefully, helping to slip his arm out of the sleeve so his sweater is tucked around his neck to give her room to investigate. "I kind of want to do an X-ray, Parker. This looks like you could have a broken rib or two."

Parker stares her down. "Mandy, be serious."

"Parker, broken ribs can give you a punctured lung."

"What will I get when they're just bruised?"

"Less bed rest," Mandy quips.

Parker gasps and narrows his eyes. "You don't have the authority—"

"Fuck you, I do." Mandy narrows her eyes in return. "You think if I called Hayden right now and told him—"

"Excuse me," I say, interrupting them both. Mandy swings

her head toward me as if she forgot I exist. I clear my throat and give her a nod in permission. "He'll do the X-ray."

Parker's jaw clenches but he doesn't argue. Mandy's smile is wide and knowing when she looks between us, but thankfully she keeps her mouth shut. The next ten minutes are full of helping to arrange Parker around in a back room that contains an X-ray machine and what looks like surgical equipment. He hands me his glasses and I hold them carefully to avoid getting smudges on the lenses.

"This is just for instances like this. When it's really bad, like it was for Reid and Dante, we meet Eric at his hotel downtown," Mandy explains to me from behind the protective wall. I can see Parker standing against the other wall with an irritated scowl, but he can't see us. The X-ray appears and Mandy leans forward with a relieved sigh. "Well, fuck me. It's not a break. Probably just a handful of painful contusions causing the bruising and swelling. He still needs to rest for at least a few days. Can you make him do that?"

I swallow hard. "Yeah."

"I'll tell Hayden and he can hate me for it."

"Are you employed by Robin? How does this all work?"

Mandy's mouth twists at the corner, in a part grimace, part smile. "It's all a little complicated. Yeah, I was recruited, so was Eric. But we're basically just on-call secret keepers for them. They have a lawyer too, in case of emergencies, but we never see her. Thankfully."

"I hope I never meet her."

Mandy snorts. "That's the spirit. You're getting it. Want to prank him or be nice?"

"Nice," I murmur, feeling soft and gooey inside for Parker.

"Cute. That's your man, huh?"

I can feel my face flush to the roots of my hair. "I think so, yeah."

"Double cute."

Mandy walks around the wall to stand in front of an irritated and tired-looking Parker. "You're lucky as hell, kid."

"Told you," Parker replies with a huff.

"Better safe than sorry. You want a cinnamon roll to go?"

Parker looks a little mollified at the offer. "Yes, please."

I hand Parker his glasses and he slides them on with a grateful smile. We follow Mandy out to the kitchen, then accept two to-go containers and a cup of coffee for Parker. When we load into the car, Parker's phone vibrates, and he tugs it out of his pocket with a wary sigh.

"Care instructions, five days of rest at a minimum. Great. Hayden will be thrilled. I won't take anything stronger than some Aleve, so do you have that? And maybe ice packs?"

"I've got all of that. Let's just get you home."

"I'm not tired."

"You are a *bad* patient, for your information."

Parker grimaces and turns to look out the window. I take a few steadying breaths to calm my fraying nerves, my worry about Parker—about everything—eating away at me. By the time we pull up to the house, I've worked myself into an anxious mess. I was doing *so* well.

"Mason?" Parker calls, voice soft and worried.

"I just need a second." I tighten my hands on the wheel, squeezing my eyes shut tight to tune everything out. "It's just a lot."

"The injury? I can go stay with the guys until I'm better."

"No, not the injury."

I glance over at Parker to find his eyebrows furrowed, a

small, handsome-as-hell frown on his face. Why does he look hotter when frowning?

"I just... I killed my uncle, and then you moved in with me and you're *always* so fucking hot, like, literally the hottest man in existence I think, and you kissed me, we kissed, and it felt good, it felt great, but also now I'm a double killer and I really actually kind of liked it, and I liked how you looked at me after I killed that guy but I also really like taking care of you and making sure you don't do anything stupid but... We kissed."

Parker looks at me so calmly, with absolutely no irritation at all about the weird, rambling tirade I just fumbled my way through. He always looks at me with that same fond expression.

"Yes, we kissed," Parker agrees, a small smile on his plush lips. "And we're boyfriends."

"Oh."

"Yeah."

"Are you sure?"

Parker's frown returns. "What do you mean, am I sure?"

"I just mean... Well... I'm a man but also I'm kind of a lot, not in the way that Reid is a lot but in the way that I am not sure I'll ever be able to go to a crowded concert or get on an airplane or eat at a buffet..."

"I am not remotely interested in any of those things," Parker says. "But what I am interested in is *you*."

"Oh," I say again like a total idiot.

Parker smirks. "Yeah."

"Okay, well. I'll just worry about the being-a-killer thing, I guess."

"I wouldn't worry about that either. I'm taking care of it."

Parker hops out of the car, clutching his ribs, before I can even work up a reply. I hop out and chase after him, but I catch up easily because he's still toeing off his shoes on the front mat when I walk in.

"What's that mean?"

"Just that you've nothing to worry about."

"About killing my uncle?"

Parker hums absently and heads toward the kitchen, where he starts the now familiar routine of making us tea. The man moves around with all the ease of someone who's always lived here, always belonged. I'm struck with the knowledge that I'm not sure I'll be able to let him go when the time comes. What will I do when he moves back to the other house? I'm *used* to him here now, and it's been nice not being alone anymore. Having Reid here had been difficult most of the time because of his antics and misbehaviors, but at the end of the day he'd *been* here. I'd liked feeling like someone else was here.

"You're not going to tell me anything, are you?"

Parker hums again. "Probably not."

"But we're boyfriends."

"Oh?" It's Parker's turn to be confused it seems. "Are we?"

I square my shoulders. "To me, yes. You kissed me."

"You said that a few moments ago."

"Kisses mean something."

"Do they?"

I grit my teeth because suddenly he's being infuriating. "To me they do!"

Parker sets the kettle on the oven with a level of calm that pisses me off. I watch as he rummages around in the cabinet to find the ginger tea he's been making for us lately. It settles my nerves and my stomach, which is a nice two for one. Once the kettle whistles, Parker pours the boiling water into two clean mugs pulled from the cabinet, then washes his hands twice before tearing open the tea to place the bags in the cups. He then sits calmly down at the table, pushes the cup across to me, and waits for me to take a seat. Okay. What's going on?

"Sit down," Parker says, tone brooking no argument.

I sit down immediately, but with a slight huff to show my displeasure. Parker just grins.

"You need to decide now how much you want to know. Do you want to be all in and know all of our business, or have a level of plausible deniability that'll keep you out of jail if everything goes south?"

"Oh."

Parker smiles placidly. "Yeah, oh."

"We kissed."

"Yes."

"I'm all in."

"Oh," Parker says in clear surprise.

"We keep repeating the same three words. Is this how arguments between us will always go?"

Parker dances his finger across the rim of his mug as he avoids my gaze. "I'm not one for arguing."

"Me neither. Reid burned all the arguing out of me over the course of his absolutely awful teenage years."

"I'm sure," Parker replies with an eye roll. "Okay, well, I killed Senator Hyland."

Suddenly the air is punched out of me. "I'm sorry, what now?"

Parker takes a sip of his tea and looks at me over the mug. Everything tilts a little sideways. "Yes, that was me. But I made it look like a suicide. Which was my plan with your uncle as well."

"You..."

"Yeah."

"Oh." I press my hand to my forehead, suddenly a little overwhelmed and kind of dizzy. "That's... Have you killed other high-profile people. I know your kill count but... I am not sure I want to know the answer to this question."

Parker sucks at his teeth. "I'll let you consider that one before answering."

"Right. You need to kiss me, right now."

Parker looks startled. "Why? Also, what about the mouth-wash and toothbrushing?"

"Because it'll distract me, I think, from having an anxiety attack. And right now, none of that shit matters."

"You're not selling it real hard here."

"Shut up and kiss me, Parker Chambers."

Parker lurches across the table to plant his mouth on mine. It's a closed-mouth kiss and a little painful, but my brain shuts right off. I all but climb the table to move toward him, and he spreads his thighs to make room for me to stand in front of him, his hands tentatively going to my hips. Our lips work together to soften the kiss through teamwork, his lips moving over mine to gentle my nerves like I'm a fright-ened foal. Which I guess in a way I kind of am.

"Mason," Parker whispers against my mouth.

I only moan and press in closer, until his tongue swipes against my bottom lip in invitation to be let in. All I can focus on is Parker, the movement of his mouth against mine, the fresh, clean smell of him, the tender touch of his fingers that hesitate for permission to touch my bare skin as they dance along the hemline of my shirt.

"Do it," I beg on a groan.

Parker doesn't ask if I'm sure, doesn't second-guess me, he

just slips his hands under my shirt against the small of my back, effectively branding me as his own. I want to climb into his lap and feel his hard cock under my ass. I want to rut against each other until we come in our pants, because my own cum doesn't freak me out at all, so I think that would work. But I also think he's a closet romantic, and I'm not sure he wants to frot with me for the first time after an argument, while drinking tea, with me using him to shut my brain off.

"Okay," I mumble against Parker's slack mouth. I pull far enough away that we're just breathing each other in. The view from this angle is delightful because all I see is Parker's blown pupils, kiss-wet lips, and stubbled cheeks. "My brain just said I should ride you until we both come in our pants, but I think maybe that's better for another time when your ribs aren't bruised and we didn't just argue?"

Parker's eyes darken. "My ribs are fine."

"Parker." I say his name like a reprimand.

"Fuck me." Parker dips his head forward to tuck his face into the crook of my neck. I loosen my hands from his shoulders to tangle them in the loose hair at the back of his neck. His hair is so soft, silken-fine, and it does something to all those touch-starved sensory receptors in my brain. "You're petting me like a dog."

I pause my petting. "Is that okay?"

Parker grunts. "Don't stop. It distracts me from how you just said you wanted to ride me until we come in our pants."

"Well, I do."

"Shhhhh." Parker's fingers tighten against my hips hard enough to bruise. I like it, more than I should. "I kind of want to—"

The doorbell ringing interrupts Parker's sentence. I *really* want to know what he was going to say. But instead, I disentangle myself from his lap and rush toward the front door. Jacob's imposing figure fills the doorway, but then Reid peeks around the side of him with a half smile, half glare. Oh no.

"Where's Parker?" Jacob asks.

The loud groan from inside the kitchen is all Jacob needs to hear to gently push past me—without touching me—to find his brother. Reid plops his hands on his hips and glares at me.

"You look rumpled," Reid notes.

I hurriedly run my fingers through my hair. "I was helping Parker get settled since he's injured."

"Settled," Reid says with lots of forced air quotes.

I narrow my eyes. "Are you implying something, Reid?"

Reid deflates as if he's been properly reprimanded. "Just wanted to make sure you were okay. And that my archnemesis is fine."

"Parker is not remotely your archnemesis, and he's fine. You can come in and check if you'd like."

I step aside so Reid can come in, smiling when he immediately takes off his shoes. We walk into the kitchen to find Jacob kneeling by Parker with a worried frown. They stop their murmuring when we walk in but Parker looks a little calmer now, which is probably a good sign of him being willing to accept care.

"Hayden was going to come but he's awful when one of us is injured, so he stayed behind. Parker says he'll stay here and you'll make sure he gets rest?" Jacob asks with a knowing little smile.

"Yes."

"Reid?" Jacob says with a lift of his eyebrow.

"Right." Reid jogs back toward the door and returns with an insulated bag. "Jacob and I made Italian penicillin. It was this soup our mom always made when we were sick, so I mentioned it once and Jacob wanted to learn. Anyway." Reid holds the bag out to me like it costs him millions of dollars to be kind. "Mason knows how to reheat it."

"Thank you, Reid," I say with real emotion. "Mom's pastina fixes everything."

"Well, it's probably not as good as hers was," Reid argues, looking severely uncomfortable.

"I'm sure it's better," I say.

Jacob stands and shoots me a wink. "Definitely since I helped. If Parker stops listening, let me know and I'll come back to put him in his place."

Parker grumbles something that makes Jacob snort, then let out a deep belly laugh. I get the feeling Parker is a notoriously bad patient. There are so many questions I want to ask them, like how they got involved in this murder-for-good business. I want to ask how many men Jacob has killed to see if it's as high as Parker's kill count. For some strange reason, I like the idea of Parker having killed the most men because in an odd way, it makes me feel even that much safer with him.

"Where's Dante?" I ask Reid as I walk them back toward the front door.

"Working with Hayden."

I lift an eyebrow. "Oh?"

Reid waves a hand. "Internal stuff, I guess. They only bring me into the loop when it's time for a mission, and those are paused until caveman back there is healed up. No missions without him, I guess."

"'Cause we're all walking grenades without Parker," Jacob says out of the corner of his mouth. He skewers me with a look as he stands halfway out of the front door. "Seriously, if he refuses to rest, call me and I'll come back. But I think he will, considering his incentive."

Huh? "What incentive?"

Jacob snorts. "Amazing, there's two of you."

I watch as Jacob jogs down the steps, then pauses at the bottom for Reid. This tentative friendship between both men is endearing and cute. It's obvious to see how much Jacob cares for Reid even in the small moments like this, just waiting for him at the bottom of the stairs. Reid does that painful little half smile he makes when he's attempting to have an emotion. I bite back a grin at the sight of it.

"You're okay?" Reid asks, sounding a little unsure.

I nod. "Yeah, I'm all right." I glance behind me toward the kitchen, finding Parker leaning back in his chair with his eyes closed. "Better than all right, I think."

"Well, I made the soup with love, so you better eat it."

"Promise."

Reid's smile turns genuine, even a little shy, before he lifts his hand to tap his nose. I'm not sure what comes over me, what powers have blessed me for the day, but instead of copying the movement, I lean forward to wrap him in a hug. He doesn't smell like cigarettes anymore; instead, he smells fresh and clean, and his hair that's auburn at the roots is a little damp from a shower. Oh, Reid. His breath hitches a little as I clutch him tight for a brief moment, then let go once it starts to feel like too much for me.

"I love you, Reid."

"Gross," Reid says with a wrinkle of his nose.

I sigh. "All right."

Reid grimaces, then mumbles, "I love you too."

"Have you ever thought about therapy? It might help. It's helped me."

Reid just rolls his eyes. "If you think Dante hasn't already coerced me into therapy, you're crazy. We *both* go. And then he rewards me with some very strenuous lovemaking."

Disgusting. But good for them, I guess.

Jacob salutes me once Reid joins him at the bottom of the steps, then I watch them disappear toward their house, catching Reid turn around once to look back at me to ensure I'm still watching. Once they're too far gone for me to track, I return to the house and lock the door, turning the alarm system back on.

"Want some of the pastina? It's so good."

Parker grunts in agreement with his eyes still closed tight. I run my fingers through his hair, smiling when he tips farther into my touch. He's just as touch starved as I am. Both of us are in desperate need of tender care. The pastina is still warm thanks to the insulated bag they dropped it off in. After filling two bowls, I place one bowl with a spoon in front of Parker, then sit with my own bowl at the table, beside him this time.

He blinks his eyes open and gives me a strange look.

"This way I'll be close if you need help," I explain before taking a big spoonful of the pastina. Oh. It *is* better than Mom's. She made this so much when we were little, and often when I was in the worst of the chemotherapy. It was basically the only thing I could keep down for a few weeks. "Eat, come on," I urge him.

By the time I'm halfway done with my soup, Parker has inhaled his entire bowl. Jesus. Before I can tell him no, he's standing to wash his dish at the sink and place it into the dishwasher. He rummages through the cabinet like he lives here, then pulls out a bottle of standard pain reliever I keep on hand. He downs three of them dry before grabbing a bottle of cold water from the fridge.

"I'll be in bed," Parker says tiredly.

Once I finish my pastina, I wash my own bowl. Climbing the stairs to join him in my bedroom, I'm confused to find no Parker. Worry slashes through me for a moment. I force myself to take a calm breath and seek him out in the guest room. He stands there with some clothes in his hand.

He looks up when he hears me come close. "I was just grabbing some things to keep in your room."

"Just move it all into my room."

Parker stares at me. "Mason, that's a little—"

"I want you there."

His jaw firms up. "You might not want me there *every* night, so no, I'm not going to move my stuff in there just yet. But I'll stay in there while it feels like I've been sent through a meat grinder, okay?"

That's acceptable. "All right."

"And once my entire body doesn't feel like one giant bruise, you're going to ride me until we come our brains out, okay?"

A hush falls over us. All I can do is nod, and Parker looks far too pleased at my reaction. I move aside so he can pass by me, obviously tired and worn out. Instead of going to the bed, he goes into the bathroom. Looking at me over his shoulder, he lifts an eyebrow in question.

"Should I brush my teeth?"

I feel my face flush with warmth and all I can do is nod. He takes off his glasses first, setting them on the edge of the vanity. Parker painstakingly brushes his teeth like he did the night before, like he's going to be inspected. Once he's done, I brush my teeth to return the kindness. While I do that, Parker turns the shower on and then steps into the shower gloriously naked, the firm muscles of his butt making dimples appear at the top. I've never brushed my teeth faster.

Steam fills the bathroom, making everything hazy and very sexy. My heart pounds with the thrill of desire, not anxiety, and it's such a welcome change that I feel a little dizzy with it. When I step into the shower, Parker's standing under the water with his head tipped back, looking so sexy and beautiful that my mouth dries.

"Maybe in the shower jizz won't freak you out?" Parker asks, voice husky.

Pictures flash through my brain of my cock in his mouth, his cock in my hand, our cocks pressed together—so many vivid horny images that my dick hardens at a speed I didn't think possible. Parker's gaze flicks down to my rapidly hardening dick, then back up to my face.

"I think maybe that's a yes?"

"Let's try." I throw myself into Parker's soapy arms, slashing our mouths together with a groan from the very deepest, darkest pits of me. "I want you so much it scares me."

"Mace," Parker growls against my mouth. He deepens the kiss, licking into my mouth, making my toes curl against the slippery shower tile.

The force of my desire for Parker could bring me to my knees, but it's more likely to make me weep. Crying right now would be beyond embarrassing. Instead of focusing on the emotions, I let my brain quiet under his lips moving firmly against mine. Careful of his ribs, I wrap my arms around his neck, going up on my tiptoes so that we're even as we kiss, making him not need to bend at all. He grips my hips roughly but doesn't tug me close, just holds me like if he lets go, I'll disappear.

I pull away from his mouth to trace my fingers down his neck, his arms, then trace back up to dance them along his collarbone.

"Touching you like this... It feels like a prayer." That's the only way I can explain it. I'm not a religious man, and I didn't grow up religious, but here in the lowlight of the shower, touching Parker's shower-warmed skin, this feels as close to godliness as I'll ever get. I tap his belly with my fingers. "Can I kiss you here?"

"Oh Jesus Christ," Parker says with a moan, slamming his eyes shut as if in pain. "You're going to fucking kill me."

"I hope not." I dip down to press a soft kiss to his belly. Water gathers on my lips, and I lick it away as I stand back up. "I don't know where to start."

"Let me," Parker says darkly, his desire-laden voice sending a deep shiver down my spine. "Can I touch your dick? I'm all squeaky clean..."

I nod because I don't trust myself to speak. Parker reaches down to take my dick in his hand, and I gasp, looking between us to watch his broad palm stroke me from the base to the tip. My breath hitches painfully in my chest when he swipes his thumb over the head, gathering the pre-cum that's gathered there. I lift my gaze to his to find his eyes caught on me, like I'm the most beautiful thing he's ever seen.

"Mason, keep your eyes on me. I want to watch the pleasure crash over you."

All I can do is nod again. I keep my eyes on his deep green eyes, lost in the magnetism that's solely Parker. He squeezes me at the base, then strokes again, this time his pressure a little firmer, making me gasp and snap my hips into his hold. His teeth flash white when he grins at my pleasure.

"You feel so good in my hand, Mace. Warm and solid and

real. One day when you're ready, I'll suck you off, and I know I'll love it. Wanna know why?" Parker asks breathlessly, like he's just as turned on as I am. But I don't dare look down, not when I'm caught like a deer in headlights. "Because everything about you is sexy to me. Everything. The way you let me boss you around but have no qualms with bossing me right back. Your shock of auburn hair that never lies flat. The way you hold a gun like you were fucking born to kill, just like I was. God. I never thought someone could turn me on so much."

"Parker," I whimper as my toes curl with pleasure.

"Can you touch me too?" Parker begs, voice hitching on the words.

I hold his gaze as I reach down to take him in my hand, gasping at the hot, steel weight of him in my grip. Words don't seem to come so easy to Parker once I'm trailing my hand up and down his cock. I take my time with him, trying to parse out what makes his lips part, what makes his eyes go just a little bit narrower.

My orgasm doesn't sneak up on me like usual, instead it slams into me. I snap my hips into Parker's firm grip and gasp, eyes widening when Parker's grin grows at the sight of me falling apart. He leans down quick and sure to take my mouth in a searing kiss. He tastes like sin and joy when he gasps into my mouth, his warm semen coating my hand. Parker steps back quickly so the water rushes over us before my brain can fully process the feeling.

I blink up at him as water splashes over me, catching his gaze with my own. Caught in the pleasure still rolling over us, I see everything I need to know in Parker's gaze. I'll never question him again—his want for me, his devotion. It's there plain as day on his beautiful face.

"Oh, Parker." Tipping up onto my toes, I wrap my arms around his neck to kiss him soft and slow, a kiss at odds with the sparks of pleasure still rattling through me. "Thank you."

"I want you so much, Mason. You've no idea."

"I do," I whisper into his ear. "I want you just as much."

"I'm so tired," Parker admits warily.

"Let's go lie down."

I tenderly dry Parker off with a new towel, doing my best to avoid his painfully bruised ribs. Parker can't stop watching me, can't keep his eyes off me, and I try not to preen under his heady gaze.

CHAPTER 10

PARKER

I can't keep my eyes off Mason. His cheeks warm under my watchful gaze, but he doesn't falter in his caretaking. Once he's finished drying me off, he carefully dresses me in the new clothes I brought with us. But he stays naked as he helps me into the bed, which gives me a delightful view of his firm *could bounce quarters off this ass* butt when he digs through his drawers to find pajamas for himself.

I'm a little disappointed once his miles of gorgeous skin are gone, but any lingering disappointment disappears when Mason joins me under the covers. The warmth of him and his proximity lull me toward an afternoon nap. He pets my hair like he did earlier, forcing relaxation upon me. We smell like each other, like bodywash, and I can still taste a hint of him on my tongue. I want to keep him on my tongue forever.

"I really like you," I whisper, losing my filter as sleep comes for me.

"I really like you too, Parker, more than you'll ever know," Mason says with a smile in his voice.

I hum in contentment and snuggle down farther into the

bed. My ribs don't hurt anymore because of the medicine. I'm warm from Mason's dizzying closeness. Wakefulness never stood a chance with that combination.

———

When I return to the living, Mason is still there, slipping his fingers through my now slightly damp hair. I groan and lean into his touch, earning me a chuckle from Mason. Blinking my eyes open, I smile a dopey smile up at him, and his lips quirk into a smirk in return. Everything just feels *easier* when I'm with Mason. Touch or no touch, he calms something inside me that I never even knew needed calming.

"It's only been an hour," Mason teases.

I stretch a little, noting that my ribs are less painful, and more just achy. Tilting my head toward him, I'm rewarded with a little scratch of my scalp.

"Must've been all I needed." I squint an eye to look at his hip, finding his phone in his hand. "What're you doing?"

Mason flushes a beautiful shade of crimson. "I was listening to that *Dungeons and Dragons* podcast I love. They just released a new episode, and you were zonked out, so I figured it was a good time."

I roll over onto my back so that Mason's front is tucked perfectly against my side. Letting my hand gently rest on his thigh, I brush my thumb over the soft material of his tattered and worn sweatpants. To touch him like this, without worry about triggering him from being outside, is a dream come true. So is just sharing a bed with him. But what we'd shared in the shower had been beyond comparison to any sexual encounter I've ever had. I don't know what my label is, and it doesn't really matter to me. All that matters is that my body feels *right* when I'm with Mason.

"Can you explain *D&D* to me?"

Mason looks pensive. "If you'll do something in return."

My heart starts to race. "Oh?"

"Yeah..." Mason leans forward, lips an inch from mine. My breath catches in my lungs and my cock takes notice, starting to harden in my pants. "If you'll"—Mason dances his fingers down my face, over my chin, then lets them land on my bottom lip—"tell me"—when I part my lips to lick the pads of his fingers, he gasps, then grins in mischief—"what your favorite book is?"

"What?"

Mason kisses me softly. "What's your favorite book?"

"*The Three Musketeers.*"

Mason snorts. "Bullshit. Tell me the real book."

"Okay, well, it's kind of stupid, but when I was a kid, I read this series about boys who get sucked into this fairy world. It wasn't what you'd expect, there was a lot of danger, and the fairies were not always nice. Anyway... I really loved that series."

"Really?" Mason asks in wonder.

I squint up at him. "Yes."

"That's so fucking cute."

And then Mason's kissing me softly, the still damp strands of his hair brushing over my forehead. I reach up to caress his jaw, hesitant at first, but then I firm my touch when Mason lets out a soft, pleased sigh. I love the feel of his slight stubble beneath my fingers.

"Explain the *D&D* stuff to me," I whisper against Mason's slack mouth.

"All right." But Mason sounds like he'd rather spend all day kissing me. "Just imagine the most fantastical video game ever, but it's real life. All these people get together with these games they plan, elaborate stories and scenarios, then they act them out with monsters and magicians. It's just *fun*."

"Kinda sexy listening to you nerd out."

Mason rolls his eyes. "Sure."

I grip his chin and turn him toward me. "It is sexy. Everything about you is sexy."

"Why do you wear contacts on missions?" Mason asks, deftly swerving to change the topic.

"I'm *almost* legally blind. Robin wanted me to get corrective eye surgery, but Jacob printed out all these horror stories about people having serious side effects that terrified me, so now I just use contacts. I sleep with them in far too often." I blink sleepily up at Mason, just enjoying touching him for as long as he'll let me. "Do you like the glasses?"

Mason flushes again. Interesting. "Yeah, I like the glasses."

Noted.

We lie in bed for a while, until Mason finishes his podcast. For dinner we wander downstairs to heat up more pastina while chatting about random things like how Mason takes his eggs, the fact I taught myself to play guitar, and why *Alice in Wonderland* is so scary. By the time nightfall arrives, I'm tired all over again. And when we curl up in bed, this time Mason is a firm line along my side, and everything feels just a little easier than it did only a few weeks ago now that he's in my grips.

———

Finally, after the prescribed amount of days of bed rest—of letting Mason dote over me—I'm cleared to return to active duty. Mason joins me at the house on the fifth day and Dante slow claps when I walk in. I tip an invisible hat at him with a triumphant grin.

"The prodigal son returns," Hayden says with a teasing drawl.

"You love me, boss."

Hayden lifts one perfect eyebrow. "Do I?"

Suddenly, I'm not sure. "I think so?"

Hayden just hums and returns to the laptop that's precariously balanced on his thighs.

Dante appears in front of me with an open bag of chips and a grin. "You want some sour cream and onion chips?"

I reach out to grab some with a scowl. "You owe me this since you didn't check on me once."

"Reid reported back," Dante says out of the corner of his mouth. "Plus, you hate being babied."

"It's like the worst thing about you," Jacob agrees.

"I feel ganged up on. This is no longer a safe space." I turn to leave but Mason stops me. He nods toward the sofa, and I take a seat with a resigned sigh. "Do we at least have a mission coming up?"

Hayden hums again. "Tomorrow night."

"Can Mason come?" Everyone turns to look at me, including Mason. "I'd feel better if he was there. I don't like leaving him unprotected, you know, since I'm staying with him for the purpose of protecting him."

The twinkle in Mason's eyes makes me want to blow our cover right now, say fuck it and tell everyone, but we'd agreed to wait until the air settles. Basically, wait until Reid is most receptive to the news since his opinion of me is currently a little less than lackluster. I lean back in my usual spot on the sofa, watching like a hawk as Mason carefully perches himself on the edge of the wingback chair Reid usually likes to inhabit. But Reid is currently sprawled on the floor on his stomach, aimlessly doodling in his sketchbook.

"What are you drawing?" Hayden asks, curiously leaning over to sneak a peek.

"Parker bleeding out," Reid answers without missing a beat.

Dante leans over and smacks Reid's ass. "Hey."

"Doing that does not in any way make me want to be nice, just for your information."

The smile on Dante's face is otherworldly. Reid goes back to drawing as if he didn't just toss a grenade at him. The room is quiet as Hayden types away. The only disruption is Jacob when he wanders into the room, tugging a shirt over his head and looking very annoyed at the sight of a full living room.

"What the fuck? When was a tribunal called."

"When I sent a text message to the group chat saying a tribunal was called to discuss the mission tomorrow night." Hayden lifts his gaze to skewer my twin with a gut-twisting scowl. "Why are you just now getting dressed? You've been home all day."

Jacob shrugs. "I was lounging in my room naked."

Hayden's jaw tightens, the muscle popping so hard it looks like it could snap, but he stays quiet, just returning to furiously typing on his laptop. Mason turns his curious gaze to me and I just shrug. They've been this way for as long as I can remember, and at this point I've given up trying to apply reason to their behavior.

Jacob tosses his big body onto the sofa beside me with a

wink and a grin. He grabs the remote from the ottoman, then turns the television on with no care in the world, as if we aren't all sitting here waiting to discuss tomorrow night.

"Are you deliberately egging Hayden on?" I ask quietly for only Jacob to hear.

Jacob purses his lips, then makes a clicking noise with his tongue that has Hayden turning around to glare at him. He just makes a kissy face until Hayden goes back to his laptop, but I can see the hunch of Hayden's shoulders, the flush that rises on his cheeks and works its way down his neck. My brother is a major asshole.

I grab the remote from Jacob's hand with a scowl of my own. "Lay off."

Jacob grabs the remote back. "Fuck off."

"Hey!"

"I've got it handled," Jacob says darkly.

I know that tone. That's his evasive tone, the one that means *don't ask me or I'm going to tell you something you really don't want to know.* But what is there that I don't want to know about Hayden? Jacob and I have lived in each other's pockets since utero, and then with Dante and Hayden for almost four years now.

"All right." Hayden stands with a flourish and tosses his laptop down onto Reid's ass. "Tribunal can commence."

"Hey!" Reid complains but stays where he is. "My ass is not a table."

"Then take a seat like a reputable member of society," Hayden points out.

Reid looks effectively admonished, so he stands with a miserable scowl and takes a seat beside Jacob on the sofa as Dante stays standing, surveying the scene with a curious tilt of his head. When Reid flicks Dante off, he just grins at Reid while shoving more chips in his mouth. I'm already tired. I'd forgotten how exhausting they can all be after spending a few quiet weeks at Mason's house.

Scully comes out from the kitchen, winds herself between Dante's legs, then heads over to the sofa to plop herself in Reid's lap.

"Oh my god, she touched me," Dante says in clear shock.

Reid looks curiously at him. "She touches you all the time."

"What?"

"Mostly when you're asleep," Reid clarifies. "She likes to sleep on your butt."

"No way," Dante chokes out.

"Never mind." Hayden claps his hands to get everyone's attention. "I'm still her favorite human."

"Just let him think that," Reid stage-whispers to Scully.

"Tomorrow's mission is downtown. There's a financial investing firm that's syphoning funds from their clients and into their own pockets. We're going to tank the business so that the liability insurance they're forced to carry by the federal government will pay out to their clients."

"That's devious, boss," I say for a bit of levity.

Hayden sniffs. "I know. Anyway, I can disable the cameras, obviously, but this is a high-rise downtown with, like, forty floors, so I need the brawn to get me up there so that Reid and I can do the hacking. I've sent the blueprints to your phones."

"Homework," Jacob mumbles with clear displeasure. "I don't need blueprints if you're shutting cameras down internally."

"You will need them to know where the security guards are stationed," Hayden argues, eyes narrowing dangerously.

"No, because they get up and do their little lookie-loo walks. We'll just deal with them as we come across them."

"No," Hayden says through gritted teeth, eyes burning like the depths of hell. "You'll review the blueprints like *usual*, do you understand?"

Jacob stares Hayden down but ultimately gives up by slouching farther into the sofa. "Okay."

Hayden looks thoroughly pleased at Jacob's acquiescence. Finally, after everyone spends a few minutes looking over the blueprints on their phones, Reid lifts his hand to ask a question. This will be great.

Hayden points at Reid with a nod of approval. "Yes, go ahead, Reid."

"Can I kill someone?" Reid asks with a feral smile.

"No," Dante says quickly.

I expect Reid to argue, to tell Dante to fuck off, but instead he just grins and looks down at his phone while typing away. That look does not bode well, actually. At least from what I've come to know of Reid.

"Be back here tomorrow at eight on the dot. No earlier, no later." Hayden stares at Jacob for a moment, then disappears up the stairs.

"What did you do *now*?" Dante demands, clearly on Hayden's side.

Jacob rolls his hand in annoyance. "Existed."

"Seems worse than normal." Dante narrows his eyes. "Do you have another girlfriend?"

"No!" Jacob yells, shocking us all. Even I jump back a little. Jacob clears his throat awkwardly. "No, I don't have a girlfriend, and I'd prefer if no one asked that or mentioned it anywhere near Hayden. Understood?"

"Uh," I say awkwardly.

"Just..." Jacob stops himself with a huff and disappears into the kitchen.

Dante tips back to look after Jacob, then flops back to the flats of his feet. He just shrugs in confusion at those of us remaining in the living room. I take that as my cue. I send Mason a look that clearly says *don't worry*, and he just smiles back at me, sending those little butterflies to flight in my belly. When I pad into the kitchen, Jacob's standing by the sliding glass door, hands in his pockets and a frown on his face.

"What's up?"

Jacob's jaw tics. "Hayden drives me fucking crazy."

"That's not news."

"Too crazy."

I tilt my head at him, noting the dark smudges under his eyes, the less than perfectly styled hair atop his head. Jacob's always been so perfectly put together so that everyone just sees a shining star when they look at him. It was always easy for me to fade into obscurity when standing next to him. We might be twins, but we couldn't be more different. Jacob is outgoing and beloved by nature, but it takes a lot of work for me to be the same way. I'd rather be at home with a book, or now at home with Mason, but Jacob loves to be the center of attention.

"Did you fuck up?" I ask.

Jacob turns his face to give me a look that says it all. He did fuck up, somehow, and doesn't know how to fix it. I turn away from him to look outside, noticing for the first time that the moon is still full. That doesn't bode well for tomorrow at all. Missions usually go to shit for us when the moon is full because it makes people fucking crazy. When we're already dealing with standard crazy, we really don't need them to up the ante because of the moon.

"Remember how Mom loathed the full moon?"

Jacob chuckles. "Brings all the crazies to the emergency department," Jacob says in the perfect imitation of our mother.

"A nurse that smoked, so counterintuitive."

"She'd be proud of us, I think." Jacob shoots me a soft look that settles those clanging pieces inside of me. When the whole world is against me, I know he'll always have my back. A built-in protector, just like I'll always be his biggest fan. "She'd be proud of you."

"We're doing the best we can with what we've got," I reassure him.

Jacob lurches forward to hug me, shocking me enough to make me gasp in surprise. We're not much for hugging, but clearly Jacob needs physical affection in the taut moment, so I loop my arms around him and squeeze tightly.

"It's all right, Jake." I kiss his warm cheek. "What's wrong?"

Jacob pulls away, embarrassed, furiously wiping at his cheek as if to hide tears. I haven't seen Jacob cry since we were small children, when I broke one of his toy soldiers. He just shakes his head in refusal to answer me, so I back off and reach out to give his bicep a reassuring squeeze. The move seems to settle him back into his bones, and we smile at each other in the lowlight of the kitchen.

"Want to know a secret?" I ask softly, clearly just between us.

Jacob grins, his normal big and broad smile. "Yeah."

I shoot a look toward the living room, meeting Mason's curious gaze as he watches our entire interaction. The smile on my face hurts, and my insides go topsy-turvy when Mason grins back at me.

"I think I'm in love with Mason."

Jacob chokes on his spit. He bends over and I awkwardly pat his back until he stands up to stare at me in confusion.

"That's not what I expected at *all*."

I shrug, helpless. "Sorry."

"Really?"

I splay my hands out in a *what are you gonna do* sort of gesture. "Something about him fits with the broken puzzle piece inside me. Does that make sense? You're not mad, right?"

Jacob looks confused now. "Why would I be mad? I'm bi!"

Okay, well. "Well, not about that part. That it's with Mason. After I made that whole *can't hook up* rule."

Jacob looks thoughtful for a moment before shrugging. "He wasn't part of the crew when you started whatever this is with him, was he? It's like Dante and Reid, I guess."

"I guess... but I won't keep you to that rule anymore. You know that, right?"

Jacob's gaze hardens again, shutting him off from me. Reid and Dante ruin the moment by stomping up the stairs giggling, leaving it just us and Mason alone out in the living room. I dare to push Jacob's boundaries and hug him tightly one more time, ignoring that small twinge in my ribs.

"See you tomorrow night."

Jacob shoves me away. "Yeah, yeah."

Once in front of Mason, I grin softly. "Let's go home."

"Home," Mason repeats, like he's just learning the word. Because yeah, his house, the one with the maroon mat by the front door, the perfectly turned coffee mugs, and the bed that smells like bodywash and lavender dryer sheets, that's my home now.

Surprise ricochets through me when I impulsively hold my hand out and Mason takes it. He twines our fingers together, until when I look down, I can't tell which hand is his and which is mine. Our fingers remain tangled on the short ride back to the house, and stay tangled as we climb the stairs, parting when we need to brush our teeth. In some way, I think Mason woke me up. Every time I had sex before him, it felt empty and meaningless, an act I had to get through to get to the other side. But with Mason, I feel more loved and wanted just in the simple act of climbing into the bed with him to fall asleep. How is that possible?

"Mason," I say softly, just when he's about to fall asleep.

Mason hums sleepily and rolls toward me, resting his warm arm across my chest. I lift my hand to trace the edge of his jaw, waiting for him to blink his sleepy ocean-blue eyes up at me. I brush the hair away from his face, needing to look into his eyes before I let sleep claim me in its clutches.

"Parker?" Mason mumbles, tongue coming out to lick at his sweet cupid's bow.

"Promise me something."

Mason curiously tilts his head against my bicep. "Yeah?"

"When you go on missions with us, always put your safety first. Don't worry about saving me or Reid. Worry about yourself. If something happened to you and I..." I stop when the emotion threatens to choke me. It's all too much. "Please," I beg without breaking his stare.

Mason swallows hard. "What are you wanting me to promise?"

"Promise you'll always come home with me."

"I promise to do my best. Is that good enough?"

I turn over to pull him into my arms, settling my arm around him like a band. Closing my eyes tight, I inhale the soft scent of his shampoo, reveling in the warmth of his skin against mine.

———

It's the night of the mission, and by the time it's almost eight o'clock, I've worried myself into a bit of a state. I try to use getting dressed as a way to get myself in the right head-space, like usual, but Mason dressing beside me has me all sorts of messed up. I don't know why, but I have this odd feeling that something's going to go terribly, awfully wrong. This is exactly how I felt the night Mason killed his uncle.

Once I'm done, I join Mason in the walk-in closet to help him put on his murder shoes. Kneeling at Mason's feet, I hold the shoes out for him to slip in, then lace them up tight so there's no room for slipping. When I'm done, I tip back on my haunches to stare up at him, and he's staring at me so lovingly that the room spins.

"Mason."

Mason reaches down to gather my hair at the top of my head, then carefully twists it into what I'm assuming is an artfully messy-looking bun. When he's done, he squints both eyes, then blows me a kiss.

"Hot like always."

"Do you have your gloves?"

Mason lifts the gloves up and waves them around. "I've got them. I also have a mask in case something gets messy and I can't stomach it."

I pat his thigh and stand. "All right, good. And you're good with your gun and taser? Like we practiced?"

With a tilt of his head, he stares up at me. "Parker, what's this about?"

Instead of answering him, I lift my hand to ghost my fingers over his cheek. "Can I kiss you?"

Mason lifts onto his toes to press his mouth to mine. I keep the kiss soft, wanting to burn this moment into my memory to hold on to forever. But I can't kiss him forever, so I pull away from him centuries too soon.

When we arrive at the house, the others are ready and waiting to climb into the car. Mason sits up front again, with the rest filing into the back, Reid happily sitting on Dante's lap. The heart of downtown takes some time to get to since Eastport University is on the outskirts, but I navigate my way through the city streets with ease, following laws to not blow our cover before the mission has even started.

It's after nine by the time we park a few blocks away from the high-rise we'll be infiltrating. Everyone jumps out of the car, but I lock the doors to give myself a moment of privacy with Mason.

"Remember what I said."

Mason rolls his eyes. "Parker, really, you're getting a little—"

"Please," I say, interrupting him. He turns to look at me in the dark of the car, eyes full of worry now instead of the annoyance from a moment ago. "Please, just stay behind me if you need to, okay?"

"All right, Parker."

"Good boy. Thank you."

Mason's lips part at the *good boy*, and I wish I had time to explore his reaction. But I'll tuck it away for the future because my anxiety is for nothing, surely. I climb out of the car, ignoring the furious glare being sent my way by Hayden, and open Mason's door for him. I help him navigate over the puddles on the ground, then join the others as we make our way toward the plaza. Mason circles his arms around himself in the crisp night air, and I wish I could tug him to me, but it's not the time. It's also probably something Mason wouldn't want, given us being out of the safe germ-free bubble of the house.

I double-check that his holster has his gun and his new taser gifted to him by Reid, then step up front with Dante to lead the charge into the office building. The lights are bright in the dark night of the city, and the others hang behind as Dante and I put space between us and them. I glance over at Dante to watch him pull the ski mask over his face, and I let out a sigh at the time I pull mine down. I *hate* wearing the masks, but sometimes we have to, if Hayden can't guarantee the camera footage will be deleted later. Also, when we leave people alive.

"Sucks having your boyfriend with you on missions, huh?" Dante asks.

The sound of our shoes slapping the shiny marble grates on my nerves and so does his question, kind of, but I know Dante doesn't mean any harm by it.

"Feels like a liability."

Dante snorts. "Sure, Parker."

"Well, how do you feel?"

Dante flashes a scary smile at the closest guard. "Like my heart stayed behind when we walked through those doors. Heyyyyy... You don't want to do that, dude. We come in peace."

"You've got thirty seconds to turn back around," the guard says in a shaky voice.

Dante makes a pouty face that would be hilarious at any other time and leans against the security counter. "Sorry, bud, but we won't be leaving. What you will be doing is taking a little nap after you tell us where your coworkers are stationed." The guard goes to reach under the counter for a button, but Dante reaches out to grab his arm in a firm, painful grip. Dante *tuts* the guard. "Don't do that, bud. You can make this hard or easy, your choice."

The guard swallows and flicks his gaze between us. "Listen, my name is Darren, and I have a wife and two daughters, they're nine and five and—"

"We're not serial killers," I say, interrupting him, already knowing his tactic. "Telling us about yourself won't stop us from tranq'ing you and making you take a nice little nap. Now, where are the other guards stationed?"

"Fifth, eleventh, twentieth, and thirty-second floor." That was easy as pie. Almost too easy.

"Nap time," Dante says before jumping over the desk, putting the man in a headlock and knocking him out. I hop around the desk myself and help Dante tie the man up with a zip tie. "So easy."

"Too easy," I mumble under my breath.

"Yeah." Dante tilts his head. "What's up, Parker?"

Unease settles heavy in my gut. "Something isn't right."

I can feel it in my bones that something is terribly, terribly wrong. Hayden leads Jacob, Reid, and Mason into the lobby, but all I can hear is the rushing of the blood in my head as I stand up. The lights to the building turn off, leaving us only in the glow of the flashing emergency lights.

"Fuck," someone says aloud.

The sounds of sirens echo around us. Fucking hell. Hayden is shocked still, but I remember the plan, and I know it well. Always protect Hayden. I have half a second to meet Dante's eyes before we spring into action. Dante grabs Reid and Mason to drag them bodily out of the building. I grab a stunned Hayden's arm and drag him along behind me, knowing Jacob will not be far behind us. It's always my job to get Hayden out, protect Hayden, and I can't focus on anything else but the mission. As long as Dante is in front of me with the brothers, it'll be okay. Jacob will be behind me.

The high-rise hallways are dark, filled only with the sound of us panting, our footsteps slapping against the expensive marble. I keep my eyes trained on the strong line of Dante's back. As we head farther down the hallway, my grip on Hayden's arm intensifies, even as he digs his feet in, making it harder to tug him along. We reach an exit door, but Dante fumbles with it for a moment, since it doesn't want to just push open. I scour the door for a sign, but Reid beats us all to it. He tugs against Dante's firm grip and slaps his hand against a small, almost hidden button against the wall that lights up in a signal that we can finally open the door.

Dante makes a relieved sound and shoves it open, tugging the brothers along behind him. My heart pounds in my ears with every step, and it keeps pounding when we break into the night air through the back door. The car is four blocks away and the lights of the sirens are getting closer, shining against the puddles on the dark asphalt. Tires screeching on gravel sets me on edge. Clenching my jaw tight, my molars threaten to crack as I use every ounce of strength to drag Hayden along.

"Jake!" Hayden shouts in terror.

But I can't turn around. Dante doesn't turn around either,

but Mason and Reid do, and I can't look at their faces because I can't know for sure what my intuition has been telling me all night. We just keep running until the sirens fade and the dark of night is all we have to guide us toward escape. All I can think about is getting us to safety, putting as much space between us and those sirens. Because those sirens mean one single thing: pain. Finally, after longer than seems possible, Dante cuts into an alleyway and guides us into an abandoned-looking restaurant that's door easily opens.

We all stand panting for a while, trying to get our breath, and Reid is the one to get his nerves about him first.

"What the fuck was that?"

"A setup," I say plainly.

Hayden screams at the top of his lungs, then turns to punch the brick wall. He comes away shaking his hand, blood dripping down his knuckles.

"Hayden," Dante says carefully, shooting a frantic look toward me while obviously trying to calm Hayden down. "Hayden, come here, boss."

"Don't call me that," Hayden murmurs in clear despair. "Where the fuck is Jacob?"

"He's the fall guy."

Hayden shoots me a glare. "What the fuck are you talking about?"

I press the heel of my hand against my forehead, urging my heart to calm, my brains to stay together, when all I want to do is fall to my knees in anger.

"Parker, what the fuck are you talking about?" Hayden asks, tone rising in hysteria. "What the fuck is a fall guy?"

"The plan has always been that if cops show up, if anyone starts sniffing around, Jacob takes the fall." I flinch when Hayden slams his fist into the wall again, only stopping when

Dante wraps his arms around Hayden and bodily pulls him away. I've never seen Hayden so angry; he's always put together, always so fucking calm in the face of the worst possible news. "Hayden, Jacob knew going in. Why do you think he followed you around?"

Hayden heaves violently and vomits all over the ground. Dante gives me a disgusted look, and I think it's because of the vomit, but when Reid grabs me and yanks me around, I know it's because I've totally fucked up.

"Hey, watch what you say, you fucking asshat." Reid shoves his fingers against my chest, boiling with fury. "Jacob protected Hayden because he *cared* for him, not because he was told to keep him safe."

"That's not—"

"Parker," Mason says, interrupting me. "Come here."

I reluctantly leave Hayden to throw his fit in Dante's arms and step over to the other side of the room with Mason. He looks sweaty and flushed, probably from the run, but also from the dilapidated old building we're in.

"Are you okay? Sorry, what do you need?"

"Parker." Mason looks so fucking sad, I don't know what to do. "Parker, are you okay?"

I blink in confusion. "Me?"

Mason steps into my space, close enough I can feel his heat, smell the calming lavender dryer sheet scent of him, and that's when it hits me. Jacob's the fall guy. All of our crimes, every single one of them, will probably fall on him. When will I see him again? When will I hug him like I did last night?

"Oh my god," I say with a choked cry.

Mason steps into my space and tightly wraps his arms around me. We're both shaking when I wrap my arms around him, burying my face deep against his neck to cry. I don't know how long we stand there holding one another. I don't know how we get back to the car, but we do. The sirens have faded, but we pass by the flashing lights on the way to the car, and my stomach turns. Is Jacob still there?

"I'll drive," Mason says, holding his hand out in demand for the keys.

I toss him the keys without a second thought. We all load into the car, me in the passenger seat and the boys each in their own seat in the back. Hayden keeps making pitiful crying noises. I feel like a total fucking asshole because all it does is piss me off. Mason is the most careful driver on the planet, hands at ten and two and going right at the speed limit. Which is the exact way someone with suspicious intent would drive.

I squirm in my seat as we head in the direction of the building we just fled from.

"Mason, there has to be a different way to get home," Dante says, voicing what I'm thinking but too afraid to say.

"This is the only way to the main state road that'll get us back home unless you want it to take over an hour and a half to get back." Mason's hands tense on the wheel. "Oh, fuck, a cop just turned around to follow me."

"Fuck." Reid glances back. "It's two cop cars actually."

"I cannot go to prison," Mason murmurs, face turning ghostly pale. "What do I do?"

The question is clearly pointed at me. I do the only thing I can think of, which is distracting him from the entire situation.

"Baby, you've just got to drive like you normally would. Want to put your *D&D* podcast on?"

Mason shakes his head. "No. No, it's fine. I'll go a little faster."

Mason steps on the gas so we lurch forward, breezing through the green light, then he turns onto the state road that'll take us home. The cops speed up and pass us by, turning on their lights as they hit the gas to head toward their next stop. Mason lets out a wary sigh and loosens his hands a little, shooting me a grateful smile.

"While I am very grateful we are not joining Jacob in federal prison at the moment, I am very curious why you just called my brother baby." Reid leans forward in his seat to shoot me a glare. "Would you like to expand on this turn of events, Parker?"

"Reid, I love you, but sit back and shut up," Mason says in a clear, commanding tone. It would probably turn me on in any other scenario, but right now it just makes me sad.

Reid sits back with a huff, Hayden lets out another mournful whimper, and Dante's gaze flicks between the two of them like a helpless puppy. I tug my phone out of my pocket like an idiot, expecting Jacob to have texted or called, but my phone is woefully silent because I'm currently with the only people who would even call me or text me.

When Mason pulls up in front of the house, everyone jumps out, but Mason doesn't move. His hands are tight around the steering wheel and his lips are a straight line.

"Mace?"

Mason clears his throat. "Listen, I need to go home and shower and take a valium because I'm extremely close to a full-blown anxiety freak-out. Am I the shittiest boyfriend on earth? Yes, because I can't even be there for you when your brother has been fucking arrested, but if I don't do this, then I'll be worthless to you."

I stare at him in shock for a moment, then swallow hard, trying to make sure I say the right thing. Mason turns his gaze to me and that's when I see it—he looks like he did that night in the hotel, like life is too overwhelming and he's shutting every function down until only the essential needs are running.

Opening the car door, I lean my head out, gaining the others' attention like I hoped. "Everyone back in the car! We're going to our house."

Reid lifts an eyebrow. "*Your* house?"

"Yeah, brat, my house. Get back in the car."

Mason makes a wounded noise. "Parker, they don't have to—"

But the guys are already piling back into the car without an argument. Mason's face flushes even in the dark, but he stays quiet, just starts the car back up when everyone is buckled in. Once he parks at the house, everyone hops out again, including me and Mason this time. I lag behind everyone to ensure they all make it in, then turn check all the cameras to calm my steadily increasing heart rate. When everything appears clear, I take a cleansing breath of relief.

Everyone toes off their shoes in a close bundle once Mason is done and flees up the stairs. I herd them to the living room like cattle, then stay them with my hands when they go to sit.

"Make sure you're clean before sitting."

Reid looks accustomed to it and carefully inspects Dante and Hayden. With a sigh, he disappears up the stairs real quick, only returning once he's found a clean flat sheet to toss over the sofa. Once done, he urges an almost comatose Hayden to sit, and Dante sits beside Hayden, pressing hard against his side.

I kneel before Hayden, but he won't meet my gaze. "I'm sorry, boss."

Hayden just purses his lips.

Dante nods toward the stairs. "Go handle Mason. I've got these two."

I stand with a weary sigh and feel actual pain at how distressed Hayden looks. But like Dante said, I've got to make sure Mason is okay now. I climb the stairs two at a time and seek out Mason in his room. His clothes are in a pile by the foot of the bed, which is unlike him, so I grab the clothes and put them into the laundry basket in the closet. As I undress myself, I close my eyes for a brief second to think of Jacob, but I try to trust the process instead of focusing on him.

The bathroom is thick with steam when I finally push in, but I'm relieved to see Mason standing under the water, not in a heap on the ground like I'd feared. When I approach the shower door, Mason glances over, eyes a little distant, but his lips still tip up slightly at the very sight of me. When he looks at me like that, I feel like a fucking king. I join him in the shower and take my hair down from the messy bun he'd done for me earlier. I should've trusted my intuition then. This entire night would be an awful premonition if I had just trusted my gut.

"Mason..."

Mason tugs me under the water and kisses me softly, light, and with no tongue, just a gentle press of mouths that makes me feel known and loved. He pulls away without a word and hands me the bodywash. After a few minutes of furious scrubbing, a sleek and slippery Mason dives into my arms to hug me, and that's when I realize he's shaking. Oh no.

"Mason," I say again.

"I'm okay." Mason lets out a pitiful little sniffle. "It's all just been soooooo much lately."

"I know."

"Jacob's going to be okay."

My fingers tighten on Mason's back for a second. "Yeah."

When Mason pulls away, his eyes are red-rimmed and puffy, making my heart ache even more. I reach up to wipe his tears away, then kiss his eyes lightly until he's sighing in satisfaction. We finish washing up, then dry off quietly in the steamy bathroom.

"I've got to go back downstairs and deal with them. You're okay?"

Mason nods while forcefully brushing his teeth. Some toothpaste slips out when he mumbles, "Took some meds already. I'm gonna go to sleep."

"Can I cuddle you in your sleep?"

Mason's eyes light up enough without words to tell me that's okay. I press a kiss to his forehead, then get dressed quickly in the bedroom. What am I going to walk into downstairs? I don't know. But I can't delay it because Hayden needs to be tended to and we've also got to figure this shit out.

I dress in sweatpants and a T-shirt, feeling beyond wrung out and tired. The lights are on when I step onto the first-floor landing. I spot Reid and Dante speaking in hushed whispers on the couch. I expect to find Hayden with them, but he's sitting outside in the dark, cradling his still bloody hand.

"Has anyone checked Hayden's hand?" I ask while standing in the middle of the living room having a slight out-of-body experience.

"It's broken," Reid says evenly.

"Fuck me."

Reid stands in a rush. "You were a *total* asshole back there, by the way. Saying what you said to Hayden about Jacob."

"It's the truth though."

Dante swears and drops his head into his hands. "You're so oblivious, Parker. Anyway, I called Mandy to see what we can do for Hayden's hand because he's going to argue until he's blue in the face about getting medical care for it. And you need to contact Alexis."

"Oh god, why me?" I *hate* Alexis. She's terrifying and she gets mad when we have legal questions, as if she isn't paid a small fortune to be on retainer for us.

"Because you're an asshole," Reid retorts. He shoves his shoulder into mine as he heads toward Hayden on the back porch.

"Hey! That's my *twin* in jail right now, you know!"

Reid aims a glare at me over his shoulder. "It should be you. You have the highest kill count."

"Reid," Dante hisses, but Reid just slides the door open with a glare and joins Hayden.

But Reid is right. It should be me in jail right now. That had been my plan if they caught on to Mason. What's any different now? I grab my phone out of my pocket when it buzzes.

"Oh fuck, it's Alexis calling *me*."

Dante gasps. "Shut up." Dante leaps up to come stand beside me, a silent show of support. I'm so screwed.

Clearing my throat, I lift the phone to my ear. "This is Parker."

"No shit it's Parker. That's who I called," Alexis sounds stern and irritated. "It's the middle of the night, you know? And your brother is in jail."

"Fuck. He called you?"

"He knows who his first call should be. Do you want to know the charges they have on him?"

I can't do it. I hand Dante the phone with a scared flourish, hands shaking at the idea. Dante takes the phone and listens to Alexis go on and on and *on* for what feels like forever.

"I understand, Alexis." Dante glances at me out of the corner of his eye, sending a shiver of fear through me. "Mhmm. Nope, we'll all stay clean while you figure Jacob out. Yes. Oh, I'll tell Parker. Thank you."

"And?"

Dante hands my phone back to me with a grimace. "She said to sit tight."

I narrow my eyes. "That's not all she said."

"No..." Dante hunches his shoulders in defeat. "She said Jacob said to tell you to remember Hayden's six. Also, he's been pinned with the Hyland and Warton murders."

The world spins on its axis.

"He's been *what*?"

Dante's big hands grip my biceps, effectively holding me up when my knees threaten to sweep out from under me. If Jacob is pinned with the murders of two senators, he's never getting out, he's never coming *home*. He has to come home. Him being the fall guy for us was never actually in the cards because we have contingencies, backups on backups, and Hayden's plans are always foolproof.

"Parker, it's all right. Alexis won't let him go to prison..." Dante trails off when I stare blankly at him.

"I have to talk to Hayden."

Dante shakes his head, clearly refusing me. "Nope, not tonight. You'll say the wrong thing and Hayden's..." Dante looks over his shoulder to where Hayden sits disassociated and distraught, injured hand hanging limply over the arm of the chair he's in. "I think we should all go to bed and figure everything out in the morning."

"You need to take showers..." I mumble, dead inside but still thinking of Mason.

"We'll figure it out. Go upstairs to Mason."

It says everything that I don't have the energy to argue.

The lights are off when I push into Mason's room, but the slight shape of him is easy to spot in the middle of the bed. I toss my shirt to the ground because I need his skin against mine to feel like I'm a real person. The moment I'm horizontal, Mason presses into me with a happy little huff that warms my broken heart. Dancing my hand up and down his spine, I tuck my face into his neck, breathing him in and listening to his quiet sleep-fueled sounds.

I protected Mason but lost Jacob, and I don't know what that says about me. I don't know what it means that I'm thankful to hold Mason in my arms, settled in my soul, but feel like a failure because Jacob isn't sleeping a few houses down. I don't know what to do, and that's not a feeling I'm used to. That's how I fall asleep, wondering if I'll ever figure out the answer.

CHAPTER 11
MASON

Last night was a shit show. I mean, how did that even happen? These guys have been doing this for years and suddenly the night I'm there on the mission, the cops show up. I'm seriously starting to develop a complex. Is this all because of *me*? My anxiety says yes, it's all my fault, Parker is going to realize I'm not worth all this trouble; he's going to drop me like hot potatoes, then blame me for the rest of his life for his brother being incarcerated in federal prison.

Groaning loudly, I pour the piping hot water from the kettle into my favorite coffee mug. The scent of spearmint and peppermint wafts from the mug in a cloud of comfort. I curl my toes into the tile to settle my errant nerves. Early morning sunlight filters in through the kitchen window, casting shadows around the tile. I take another deep breath and sip at the still too hot tea, leaning the small of my back against the counter as I stare down into the mug.

Parker would never blame me. He's not like that. But last night his brother did something none of them ever expected. All I can think to do is confess to killing my uncle myself. It would solve one problem but cause a cascade of others. I'm not sure Parker would ever let me if I tried. Plus, prison would likely kill me with the combination of inescapable germs and close quarters. My brain would never recuperate.

"Sup," Dante calls out as he pads in, hair a mess, shirt rucked up to show off his tattooed abdomen.

"Hello."

"Your brother isn't far behind me." Dante wrinkles his nose when he opens my fridge, probably because all that's in there are very healthy choices. He dips back to look at me past the fridge door. "You got any eggs? And tortilla wraps? I can make breakfast burritos."

I shrug. "I definitely have eggs, not sure about tortilla wraps. Help yourself to whatever. Just... wash your hands."

Dante winks. "Got it."

The quiet sound of Dante cooking breakfast fills the kitchen. He doesn't try to make conversation, which is exceedingly kind after the mess that is my brain this morning. I leave him to cook and take a seat at the dining table just as Reid stumbles sleepily down the stairs, hair in a million directions, eyes zeroed in on Dante.

"You're such a jerk," Reid mumbles, but he still seeks Dante out for a kiss.

"Yeah, yeah." Dante grins at the top of Reid's head when my brother takes a perfectly rolled breakfast burrito.

Reid joins me at the table while biting into the burrito. He smiles weirdly at me, then sneaks a peek at Dante as if afraid to be overheard. Leaning as close as he can without making me uncomfortable, he whispers, "Did Parker sleep in your room last night?"

"Uh."

Reid squints and finishes off his burrito. "Seriously? Why is it such a secret?"

Because Parker has the perfect timing, he descends the stairs right then, dressed for the day in sleek dress pants and a tight polo that shows off the muscles in his arms. Ignoring the other occupants of the kitchen, he stops beside my chair, resting his hand on the edge so he's not touching me.

"I took a shower and brushed my teeth," Parker says with a glimmer in his eyes.

I lean back in the chair, offering my mouth to him for a kiss. He dips down, kisses me softly, like a pair of butterfly wings over my lips, then wanders off to join Dante in the kitchen.

"You let him *kiss* you?" Reid asks, clearly shocked.

"I think my brain knows his germs and my germs are best friends. He's kind of hijacked my brain. The things I used to worry about in regard to touch don't bother me so much anymore. Only when it comes to him though."

Reid makes a disbelieving noise. "But why Parker?"

Parker looks over his shoulder at us at the sound of his name. His hair is in a loose half-bun, still wet from his morning shower, and his evergreen eyes make me feel like I'm home.

"'Cause he makes me feel safe."

Reid pretends to puke. "Gross. Don't call him daddy in front of me."

Now it's my turn to almost hurl. "That's disgusting. Never say that again. I would *never* call Parker daddy. Do you call Dante daddy?"

Reid looks anywhere but at me. Oh yuck.

The front door opens to reveal a sloppily dressed Hayden, his face ashen and hair a knotty mess. He pauses at the front door to take off his shoes, wordlessly padding into the kitchen to wash his hand that isn't ensconced in a neon-green cast. All of us stay quiet, eyeing him with the eagerness of children watching a parent come home late at night.

"Boss?" Dante asks before he shoves a burrito into his mouth.

Hayden clears his throat awkwardly and steadfastly avoids everyone's gazes, instead shuffling around to pour himself a cup of coffee that Dante so kindly made for everyone. The tension in the room rises a few degrees, finally lowering once Hayden sits himself down at the table opposite Reid.

Trailing his finger over the edge of the cup, Hayden blinks hard a few times, and it's such a particular, evasive maneuver that I'm not sure anyone else recognizes it for what it is but me. It's a tic. This man who appears to have it all together, who runs this crew like the captain of a well-oiled ship, is so anxious he's ticcing. I'd know because it happened to me for years before therapy and medicine brought my daily anxiety to a manageable level. But is it the weight of his leadership role on his shoulders or the loss of Jacob that's causing the severe anxiety?

"I... Uh." Hayden stops abruptly and squirms in his seat, shoulder tilting forward, then backward in a jerky, painful-looking movement. "I don't know what to do."

I meet Parker's gaze over Hayden's head, and Parker looks so distraught, so broken, that my gut tightens and hot shame rolls through me. But Parker holds my gaze, refusing to let me roil in self-pity, because just like I know deep down none of this is my fault, he knows it too. Parker's strides are sure as he makes his way toward the table, sets his mug down, then sits beside Hayden without a word.

Dante brings a plate of food over to the table, then quietly joins us all as we wait Hayden out.

Reid speaks first. "The attorney, Alexis... Dante spoke to her last night and she's on it."

Hayden lets out a bitter laugh. "He's going away *forever*. And Robin isn't answering my texts. I don't know what the fuck to do. I just..." Hayden drops his head into his okay hand, looking the perfect picture of a defeated man. "This is all my fault."

"Uhm, the blame game does no one any good." Dante reaches over to clap Hayden's shoulder. He squeezes hard once, then dips down to try to catch Hayden's gaze where it's locked on the table. "Hayden, this isn't your fault."

Hayden starts to shake his leg hard, causing the table to vibrate. "If I had... If I had done more research. If I had just listened to him when he said it felt wrong, he didn't like the setup... I just should have fucking listened to him."

"He told you he didn't like the setup?" Parker asks, eyebrows furrowed.

Hayden waves a hand. "He always did that when the mission counted on y'all backing me up. He wanted Dante and Reid to start picking up the hacking shifts."

"What?" Reid gasps.

Hayden blinks four times again, then twists his hand in a hard movement, making the joints crack. He's about to fucking break. I meet Parker's gaze again and make furious eyes at him, enough to have him looking a little fearful.

"Hayden?" I ask softly.

Hayden lifts his light blue eyes to mine, as if coming out of a daze. "Oh. Hi."

"Hi." I smile at him, the most reassuring smile I can

muster, the kind that Parker always sends my way. "How about just you and I talk?"

Parker holds out a hand to stop us from getting up. "I don't think that's—"

"I've got it, Parker," I say.

Parker quiets and clenches his jaw, muscles wound tight, and just nods in what seems like understanding. I head into the living room with a deep pit of worry in my belly. But halfway there I change directions. I head to my study on the second floor, a place I haven't been for almost a month now since I no longer have to do all the dirty work for my uncle. I open the door wide, let Hayden walk through, then softly close the door behind us. Hayden looks around for a little while, cataloguing all my books and dipping down to look out the bay windows that face the front yard. He swings back around, neon-green cast making his arm swing heavily at his side, and fixes me with a distrustful stare.

"So?"

"Are you okay?"

Hayden snorts. "I'm fine. I just need..." He clears his throat and runs a hand through his hair. "I just need to get my shit together, man."

"How's your hand?" I take a step forward to look at it, but Hayden pulls it away, clutching it to his chest. "I'm not going to touch you without your permission."

"I... I know that. I know that," Hayden repeats, a little surer than the first time. He scoffs and looks back out the windows. "Jake's going to be so mad when he finds out I broke my hand by punching a fucking wall. Livid."

"Well, we can tell him it happened when we were running away."

Hayden screws his mouth up in a scowl. "He'll know the truth. He knows everything."

"Oh?"

Hayden tics again, three blinks and a shoulder lift. "Nothing gets by Jacob."

"Do you usually call him Jake?"

"Yeah... What did you want to talk about?" Hayden asks, eyes narrowed as if he's caught on to my game.

"You just seemed really anxious. Do you have anxiety?"

"What is this? Therapy?" Hayden scoffs and starts to leave, but I hold my hand up to stop him, and he freezes right before coming into contact with my hand. He looks down at my hand in shock, then his eagle-eyed gaze swings back to me. "Oh. Mason has a pair on him."

"And you hide all your anxiety behind bravado and quips."

Hayden's smirk turns cruel at my words. He crosses his arms over his broad chest, fixing me with the kind of stare that only a few weeks ago would've had me crumbling to the ground. But after a while with these guys, I've learned they're all just young men with enough problems to stack up and make killers. But the question is... what made Hayden a killer? And why is he so upset at the idea of Jacob never coming home?

"What are you asking, Mason?"

"I'm asking if you and Jacob are in a relationship."

Hayden whistles and rolls his eyes. "Wow, you really don't know shit. You think I'm so upset because Jacob is behind bars? I'm upset because the mission is fucked and Robin isn't answering... and I've got nothing to fucking do. Besides a paper that's due in two days that I'm going to have to pull out of my ass."

"Nobody calls him Jake."

Hayden tics again, then awkwardly clears his throat. "Parker does."

That I know, but I've only heard him do it once. "Does he?"

"You know... You don't get much insight from Parker, do you? Makes sense, he's our silent killer. Mr. Quiet. Never really know what he's thinking."

Hayden's struck my last nerve, but I don't let him see it because I know that's what he wants. He's deflecting all the worry he's feeling onto me, trying to make it my problem. But if there's one thing I'm not going to start worrying about, it's Parker's and my relationship. If I'm secure in anything, it's Parker. The way he looks at me says it all.

"Well, you seem better than you did at the table earlier, so I'll stop prying. But we have to try to get Jacob out, if not for you, then for Parker."

Hayden tics again but leaves the study without another word. He leaves the door open, and I take a few steadying breaths once he's gone. Jacob. I pinch the bridge of my nose and squeeze my eyes shut tight in exhaustion. I don't know what we're going to do, and if Hayden has his way, we'll probably all go down in a blaze of glory. I'm not averse to more violence, but I'm definitely not in favor of any more of us going to prison.

When I exit the office, Parker is leaning against the wall with his arms crossed over his chest and a patient look on his tired face.

"Hi," I say quietly, softly smiling his way.

"Hi," Parker echoes. He looks both ways, then nods toward my bedroom at the end of the hall. "Got a few minutes for your man?"

I smirk. "Depends on what it's for. Also, I really like you saying that."

Parker quirks his head. "Saying what?"

"That you're my man."

Parker's smile turns deep and wanting, and my insides go topsy-turvy at the sight. Pleasing Parker is so easy. He never leaves me guessing and always happily takes what I'm willing to give with a thankful hand. I think Parker has been starved for love his entire life, and every ounce of love I give him nourishes him down to the bone. It's a heady feeling to give someone as rawly powerful as Parker everything he needs. Me? Just plain Mason. It'll never get old.

"I'm your man and you're mine, right?" Parker asks, clearly pleased.

I flush but hold his gaze, giving him a nod that makes him look somehow even *more* ecstatic, despite our current circumstances. Parker lets out a sigh and steps forward to tug me into his arms. I go because he's not left the house, because he's showered, because he's germ-free for the moment and so very, *very* mine. My brain is quiet and happy in his arms, my body leaning against the strength of his with an ease I never once imagined in my life.

"We'll figure out Jacob," I murmur into the softness of his shirt.

Parker squeezes his arms tighter around me. "I know, but we've also got to figure out Hayden."

"He's... weird?"

Parker snorts. "Good word to settle on, but yeah, he's weird. Jacob seems to keep the weirdest parts of him in check."

"Is he mentally all right?"

Parker shrugs. "I've never asked him, which probably

makes me a piece-of-shit friend, but I try to make this all as easy on him as I can. He's the boss. We all know that."

"When you say he's the boss... Like, he doesn't call the shots, does he?"

Parker pulls away to rub his hands up and down my cold arms. He smiles happily when my skin warms up and pebbles under his touch.

"He's not Robin. Of that, I'm sure. Hayden is just very analytical, plus he's very black or white. To him there's no grays. Which is why he and Jacob go at each other like cats and dogs, because Jacob and I... We live somewhere in the middle. Nothing is as straightforward as Hayden would like to believe." Parker sighs in anguish, then leans his cheek against my cheek as if it's his favorite place to be. "Hayden is going to want to go to war to get Jacob out."

"Don't you?"

Parker shakes his head, mussing my hair up with the movement, which makes me snort with laughter. I can feel Parker's smile in the air, the way everything lightens just enough to make me feel okay.

"I do. I'll get him home, but I'm not going to risk blowing the world up to do it. Whereas Hayden will want to go nuclear."

"I asked him if they're in a relationship."

Parker pulls away with wide eyes. "You what?"

Lifting my hand, I caress Parker's unshaven jaw, enjoying the feel of the stubble against my palm. He's wearing his glasses, which always makes him look so soft. "He called him Jake last night, and Jake again when we just spoke. Does that mean anything to you?"

Parker frowns, then looks behind us, gaze locked on something down the stairs. When he turns back to me, his eyes are watery. I feel like I've misstepped somehow, made a grievous mistake just by mentioning the nickname, but then Parker dips down to kiss my brain into silence. He backs me up against the wall, cupping my jaw in the palm of his hand, tipping my head back to kiss me exactly how he wants. I gasp into his mouth, then shiver with my entire body when he presses his thigh against my groin.

"Parker?" I mumble against his mouth.

"I love you," Parker says, voice thready, lips still delightfully moving against mine. "I'm fucking in love with you, and I don't want to wait one more second not saying it because if something happened to either of us without me ever saying those words, I think that'd be the biggest travesty of all time."

I stare at him in shock, which is the worst move of all time because Parker looks a little terrified of all the words he said, and even more terrified when I stay silent. Words escape me though, so I'll have to show him another way. I grab his face and pull him to me, kissing him with all the emotion I've built up over the past few weeks. He tastes like Parker; not toothpaste, not mouthwash—he just tastes like him and also a hell of a lot like *mine*.

"Do you... Do you?" Parker asks against my mouth.

"I love you too. I think you're my puzzle piece."

Parker snorts and kisses me harder, his laughter pouring into my mouth like its own type of medicine. My nose clanks against his glasses, so he pulls away to tug them off, but I stay him with a hand on his neck. A curious smirk tilts up the side of his mouth, but he just pushes his glasses up higher and continues to kiss the air from my lungs.

We kiss for so long that my lips feel numb when he finally pulls away. I reach up to fix his hair, tugging the tie out and twisting his hair back up into a little bun with a few strands hanging loose. His eyes are tender and raw as he watches me take care of him.

"I want to—"

The doorbell rings before Parker can finish his sentence. Why are we always being interrupted? Parker kisses me once more on the mouth, then grabs my hand and drags me down the stairs. Dante and Reid are sitting at the kitchen table, eyes turned toward the front entrance. Hayden stands in the backyard, casted arm slung over his head as he stares out at the yard like it contains all the answers to the universe.

"I'll get the door, you can sit with Dante and Reid," Parker says, gently shoving me toward the kitchen.

I stand firm and narrow my eyes. "I'm not going anywhere. This is my house. You can open the door if you want though."

"Mason, really, just let me be—"

"No."

Parker stares at me. I stare back at him.

Finally, Parker sighs in defeat and heads toward the door. He aims a look over his shoulder as if to say *stay*. I let him order me around and duck back a little so I'm in a good position to see who's at the front door. Parker opens the door halfway and heaves a sigh of relief. He swings the door open to reveal a tall woman with a jet-black bob and a hot-pink pencil skirt with a matching blazer. She shoves past Parker to look around the house, almost takes a step in, but Parker grabs her arm roughly.

"You've got to take your shoes off," Parker orders, voice firm and brooking no argument.

The woman balks. "These are Jimmys."

"Off," Parker repeats.

"Madness," the woman gripes, but she toes off her black heels so that her feet are bare minus her stockings. "Better?"

Parker nods in acceptance. "You may proceed."

She stops in front of me with a curious look. "Who are you?"

"I'm—"

"This is my boyfriend," Parker tells her, eyes sharp as he comes around to take my hand in his firm grip. "He's part of the crew now."

"All righttttt..." The woman lets out the loudest sigh I've ever heard, then looks around the room. "Where's the blond one?"

"There are two of us now," Reid yells out, but he stands and heads toward the back door anyway.

"I forgot." She turns back toward me and offers her hand. "I'm Alexis, the attorney who keeps them all out of federal prison."

I smile blandly at her. "I have a germ thing, so sorry if I don't shake your hand..."

Alexis yanks her hand back as if she's been burned. "My bad." She surveys the room, then strides into the kitchen with all the confidence as if she's still wearing her four-inch heels. Dante shrinks a little the closer she gets, fear and admiration clearly written across his adoring face. Amazing. I let Parker take my hand and tug me along, curious to see how this is all going to play out.

Hayden comes into the room with all the subtlety of a category five hurricane. He huffs and puffs, avoids Alexis' gaze, and throws himself down at the table despite Dante's kind murmurs. Alexis looks at each of us, an aura of a mindful babysitter who's been disobeyed radiating from the very core of her. I even feel a little ashamed when her gaze lands on me.

"Okay, so they've got Jacob in custody, and they're charging him with first-degree murder for Warton and Hyland, along with a bribery charge for Hyland, as there was an email on his computer demanding money in order to stay silent about the less than savory charges we know have been levied against both men." Alexis scrolls through her phone, then taps it against her thigh while blowing out her cheeks. "I tried to get bail at the hearing this morning, but they're not considering it. They think he's a flight risk considering his charges."

"Duh," Hayden says with derision.

"And they think he acted alone."

Hayden's head snaps up. "What?"

Alexis spreads her hands in a *you got me* sort of gesture. "He hasn't spoken to them, he knows better than that. I was his first phone call. But so far, all the evidence they've mounted against him appears to show a man who acted alone."

"What's the fucking evidence?" Dante asks with a growl.

"Circumstantial at best. License plate photo for a vehicle on the highway, grainy surveillance footage, and a bullet matching the gun he had on him at arrest being found at the crime scene."

"Wait," Parker says, holding his hands out with a shaky laugh. "None of that points toward Jacob. That all points to *me*."

"Please don't confess any crimes to me right now because I absolutely cannot take it," Alexis begs while simultaneously tossing Parker an annoyed look. "You're all clearly being framed. It's not my business to know why, nor do I particularly care. I'm only paid to protect all of you by keeping you out of jail. But you've got the cops sniffing your way now, so I highly suggest all criminal activities be paused, for now." Alexis aims her final sentence at Hayden, who just looks grumpier and more annoyed as the seconds pass.

"Okay, so... you're going to get him out, right?" Reid asks.

"To quote Hayden... duh." Alexis winks at Reid, then turns her attention back to Parker. "He wants to see you. But may I remind you that all conversations held at the correctional facility are recorded. So do not go in there and implicate yourself in any way."

"What about me?" Hayden asks, tone hopeful, eyes wide.

"He did not mention you at all," Alexis says offhandedly. "But also, I believe I might be the bearer of bad news on this one, but Robin has added another member to the *keep you shits out of trouble* crew. He's outside."

Hayden looks crestfallen. "You've spoken to Robin? Since Jacob's arrest?"

Alexis rolls her eyes. "Obviously. I'm here." She stomps away from the table but pauses a few feet away to send us all the most disappointed and annoyed look I've ever seen. I want to melt into the floor. "Be quiet, keep your heads down, and absolutely, under no circumstance, are you allowed to kill someone."

She heads back to the mat by the front door, puts on her shoes, then leaves without another word. Wow. I fear her but am also a little bit in love with her take-no-shit attitude. The door opens again to reveal a broad-shouldered, barrel-chested man with light brown curls and a permanent-looking five o'clock shadow.

"What the fuck!" Reid screeches. He's halfway across the table before Parker grabs his legs and tugs him back. "Let me at him! I'm going to chew through his chest, eat his heart, then spit it out into his mouth and make him eat it!"

Hayden's eyes go wide, and he starts to laugh hysterically. "Oh my god, this takes the fucking cake. Robin hired you? I'm going to go kill myself. Goodbye."

"Everyone shut the fuck up!" Parker yells. He tosses a look full of vitriol toward a still seated Dante. "Handle your bulldog, will you?"

"Uhm, if Reid doesn't kill him, I will, so you need to decide who is going to jail for first-degree murder beside Jacob." Dante delivers the sentence with an air of finality that sends a shiver down my spine. "Reid! Stop squirming on the table. You look ridiculous, baby."

Reid flips over onto his back and shoots a lethal glare at Dante. I can't help but laugh because it's so reminiscent of when he'd glare at me when I'd first gained custody of him. Back then we were just kids, how had I ever been deemed fit to parent him as barely twenty myself. My laughter must be louder than I realized because Reid tips his head back to aim that terrifying glare at me.

"Shut up! He's the man who tortured me, Mason."

I swing my head back to the new addition to the room. All the blood in my body boils and my heartbeat rushes in my ear, the sounds of everything around me disappearing until all I can see is a funnel of violent crimson that zeroes in on the man who tore my brother to bits. Forgetting about germs, about touch, about *anything*, I lunge across the room but don't make it far enough to make contact with the intruder. Parker's arms wrap around me tight, squeezing me to him, even as I keep trying to escape his grip.

"Mason," Parker says gruffly into my ear as I try to lunge

at the oddly grinning man standing with a self-satisfied smile in my entranceway. "Alexis said it was fine."

"He turned Reid's stomach into ground beef!"

The man lifts one hand. "I was paid to turn your brother into ground beef. It was not because I wanted to, do you understand?"

Reid screams behind me, and Parker just squeezes his arms tighter around me, enough to make me focus on him and nothing else.

"Excuse us for a moment," Parker says with false cheer.

"Okay."

Parker drags me backward toward the backyard, where Dante is already wrangling an extremely pissed-off-looking Reid. If I didn't know better, I would think Reid was going to bite. Hayden follows us all outside with a bored sort of look, that damn neon cast hanging limp at his side.

"You guys put on a fun show, little psychos." Hayden tosses himself into a chair and stares up at the sky in exhaustion. "Robin hasn't said anything, but Alexis said Claude is legit so... we go with it." Hayden turns his head to fix me and Reid with a stern stare as our boyfriends hold us tight. "Can your minders let you go or are you going to commit a felony against that kind Russian in there?"

"Kind!" Reid exclaims in shock. "I'll show you fucking kind! He tore me to pieces!"

Hayden rolls his eyes. "And now we must play besties. Well? Can you both behave?"

Reid goes to make what I assume is another snipe, but I whistle out of the corner of my mouth, forcing him to turn my way. We stare at each other for a fraught moment before I lift my arm over Parker's to sweetly tap my nose. The corner of Reid's mouth quirks up in a frustrated tilt of a smile.

"Jeez, Mason, teach me your ways," Dante says with a smile.

Reid elbows him in the ribs, making him yelp and let Reid go. "You did not defend my honor."

"I was too busy ensuring you don't go to prison, sue me."

Reid gives Dante the stink eye, then warily joins Hayden at the seating area. Parker is not so quick to let me go. He grips my chin, tilting my face so he can look into my eyes. That smile I love so much covers his face, making me feel safe and secure in the circle of his arms.

"You gonna be okay, baby?"

"I won't murder him, I promise."

"No bodily harm either," Parker amends with a proud smirk.

With a pained sigh, I tilt the rest of the way to press my lips to his and kiss him softly in promise to not inflict bodily harm onto Claude. Although I want to, very badly. But if anyone deserves to be able to, it would be Reid, so I'll leave that up to him.

A knock on the sliding glass door grabs all our attention. Claude is standing on the other side with a terrifying little smile, one hand tucked into the front pocket of his jeans, the other resting on the glass like a bored child being asked to be let back inside. Jesus. Who is this guy?

Hayden clears his throat and gives Parker a look I can't parse, but Parker clearly understands because he lets me go, taking a moment to guide me into a chair beside Hayden. Again he pushes me down, with a look that clearly says stay, and I obey again because Parker usually knows best. I watch with bated breath as Parker heads to the door, slides it open, then invites Claude out with a flourish of his hand.

"You're here because the boss says so," Parker says with a

nod toward Hayden. "But if you touch Reid, that one will kill you"—he points toward Dante with a severe look, then he points at me with the scariest smile I've ever seen—"and if you touch him, you'll die twice, because I'll kill you, bring you back to life, then kill you again to make sure you end up in the very last circle of hell."

Claude holds up two fingers in a Scout salute, which is laughably unbelievable for some reason. "No touching."

"Actually," Parker amends, "don't look at Mason either. You can speak to me."

"Okay, you are all children. I am not touching any of you. Puke. Gross. Nasty children. I am here because your benefactor has hired me full-time! I am now on the payroll like all of you." Claude does jazz hands and grins like a maniac, sending a shiver of fear rolling through me. "I am here because one of you is in jail for bad crimes, yes?"

Hayden stares at Claude, then starts laughing hysterically like he's heard the funniest joke of all time. He lifts his good hand to his eyes and squeezes, and Parker shrugs at me when I look at him for help. Once he's done laughing, Hayden lets out a little whistle and leans his head back against the chair once again.

"I'm going to need to be sedated to survive this," Hayden says, voice thin and shaky.

"Boss?" Dante asks, voice just south of tender.

Hayden sighs loudly and rolls his head again to look at Claude. "So, how are you supposed to help us get Jacob out of jail?"

"I am not helping you get him out of jail. I am helping you track down the people who are sabotaging him. Because we all know Parker killed the first senator, and the little redhead psycho killed his uncle." Claude grins at us all, blinking his eyes in a cloying way that makes me feel a little ill. "Right?"

"What made you come to that conclusion?" Parker asks with perfect political correctness.

Claude snorts in obvious derision. "If you think no one knows what you are doing... you are delusional. That is why I gave that one so many scars, yes?" He points at Reid, who narrows his eyes with a glare so defiant and angry, I feel it in my bones. "Now, we should probably all get to work. It will take much effort to get the twin out of jail. They want to bury him."

"But why?" I ask with a quick look around the room. "I don't understand why they'd pin it on Jacob?"

Claude shrugs and pouts. "He was the one left at the scene. If it had been you, they would have pinned it on you."

Hayden swears before leaning forward to drop his head into his uninjured hand. Dante makes an awkward sort of face, then leans over to grip Hayden's shoulder tight, shaking a little in an obvious effort to make Hayden feel less alone. I get the odd feeling that we're all missing something. There has to be a piece of the puzzle to tell us *why* someone has decided to implicate Jacob in a crime he didn't commit. Especially if someone knows that it was actually Parker and me.

Wait.

"I sent all that dirt on senators and congressmen, even certain business owners, to my uncle," I say, thinking out loud more than anything. Everyone turns to look at me, including a harried Hayden. I rub my hands together awkwardly before continuing. "Maybe... Maybe all of that would be of value to someone and they would protect us. Maybe we just need to find the right buyer?"

Claude claps. "Finally, I can be of use. Give me an hour."

Claude disappears back to the front door, carefully slips his shoes on, then steps outside before any of us can ask a single question. Hayden makes this scary animalistic wounded noise that has us all starting in our chairs. His hands shake when he stands and descends the steps to stand in the winter-dead grass. I watch as he curls his toes into the ground and lifts his arms to rest atop his head, like he's praying to some earth god to help him solve this wild problem.

"Hey," Parker says, resting his hand on my thigh. "It's all right."

"Yeah, but... something isn't adding up. We're missing something. If they *know* it was you and me, why are they pinning it on Jacob?"

Parker's smile is bittersweet. "Because he's *letting* them, baby. He's letting them."

"I just don't understand."

"You good down here?" Parker asks Dante.

"Yeah, I got it," Dante reassures Parker with one of those crooked little smiles of his. "Hayden and Reid are easy to handle."

"Fuck off." Reid promptly stands up and scurries down the stairs to speak to a stricken-looking Hayden.

Parker takes my hand in his and drags me inside the house. The strong line of his body is so familiar to me now, synonymous with strength, safety, and home. Does he feel the same way about me? Actually, I know he does, because it's in the way he thinks of me before anyone else. How he zeroes in on me whenever we're in a room together.

Parker is on a mission, his strides sure and deliberate as he goes up the stairs and into the bedroom. He stops once we're inside and turns around, moving past me to gently close the bedroom door with a soft *snick*. My pulse leaps up slightly at the sight of his hands pressed to the door, fingers tense, arms a solid line as he very desperately clings to his control.

"I need to drown it all out, and I want to continue our conversation from earlier," Parker says seriously, voice pitched low, sending a shiver of desire right down my spine. "But I know you're anxious... I don't want to overwhelm you—"

"I want you." I swallow loudly, and it echoes around the room. "I *always* want you, Parker. And I feel like shit is about to get so out of hand that my anxiety will be too high to try anything at all beyond this, but I want to be as close to you as a human being can be, and I want to hold you every night, and I just want *you*."

"Please fucking tell me I can kiss you," Parker begs, sounding beyond wrecked.

My hands shake as I reach for him. "Kiss me, oh my god."

And then Parker is on me. Slipping my fingers into his hair, I undo his messy bun so that I can tangle my fingers in the silken strands of his hair, hanging on as he backs me up toward the bed with very obvious intentions. I tumble onto the bed, a laugh rattling out of me as Parker hurriedly rips my pants off.

He stares down at me, his chest rising and falling as he breathes through his desire. I watch, entranced, as he presses the heel of his palm to his cock, letting out a groan that makes my own cock fill in my boxers. Parker lets out another groan at the sight of my clear want for him. His gaze snaps to mine, eyes bright and wild like an animal.

"Can I suck you? I can't stop thinking about it."

"Yes! But... condom?"

Parker nods hurriedly. "Yeah, that's fine. I just want you in my mouth."

Parker holds his hand up in the universal sign to wait and disappears from the room. When he reappears a second later, he's got a box of fancy-looking condoms, and he's ripping his shirt off with one hand over his shoulder. The move is so sexy that my mouth goes dry at the sight. I love Parker in every way, but I really love when his skin is pressed against mine.

Parker freezes. "Do I need to take a shower? Or...?"

"No, just get over here. Your germs are my germs."

Parker's grin could illuminate the deepest depths of outer space. He crawls over me to kiss my mouth like a man possessed. I gasp into his mouth when he bites down softly on my lip before he soothes the ache with his tongue, then his lips. I'm a quivering mess underneath him because he mentioned sucking me off, but when is it going to happen? What does he have in store for me before the main event? Parker trails his hand under my shirt, scratching lightly at the skin he finds there. I squirm underneath him to get more of his body in contact with mine.

"Please."

Parker kisses down my jaw, to my neck, then to my collarbone. He noses my shirt aside, then chuckles softly. "Please what?"

I huff in frustration. "I want you so bad it hurts."

"Mmm, you think so, but I can make it hurt a lot worse."

"Parker!" I shout in frustration.

Parker lifts his hand to cover my mouth with a chuckle. "They'll hear us downstairs. Be quiet. Lift up."

Parker removes his hand from my mouth and helps me sit up so that he can take me out of my shirt. The way he looks at me once I'm naked makes me feel so cherished and loved, I have to fight back a tide of emotions that would definitely ruin the moment. But Parker's eyes shimmer a little as well, and I feel a little less alone in the emotional upheaval of the moment. I sigh in wonder as he dips to kiss down my chest. His lips are pillow soft and warm, but the scratch of his stubble makes me squirm in a way that I could never put down into words.

Just before he puts his mouth on my cock, he leans back to open up a condom. He carefully rolls it down my cock, making me squirm and gasp beneath him, which only makes the infuriating jerk grin down at me.

"Mason," Parker says seriously, a stern look on his sweet face.

"What?"

Parker dips down to ghost his warm breath over the tip of my cock. I dig my toes into the comforter to gain ground when I feel like I'm steadily losing my grip.

"Remember this forever," Parker demands, just before taking my cock into the warm confines of his perfect mouth.

My hips lift off the bed of their own accord. Parker pulls off to stare at me and I mewl at the loss of him.

"Can I hold you down?" Parker asks.

I nod furiously, feeling out of my body. "Yes, yes, whatever!"

Parker only chuckles and lowers himself back down on my cock. The sensation is like nothing I've ever felt before. He's never sucked a dick in his life, but it feels like Parker has been sucking my cock for decades. He knows the right amount of pressure to make my head feel light; my limbs go tingly with the need for more. His hands hold my hips down so that I can't press up into his mouth, making the experience even more heady because despite my cock being in Parker's mouth, he's the one who's in control. After spending my entire life controlling every aspect of the world around me, knowing that Parker can handle me settles me into my bones.

When he takes my cock to the back of his throat and swallows, that's when I lose the war on my impending orgasm. I let out an earth-shaking groan and release into the condom, wishing distantly that I could come down his throat so that a piece of me is inside him for a little while. I watch, detached, as Parker pulls off my cock, dropping his forehead to my hip as he reaches down to take his own impossibly hard dick in his hand. He's bigger than me, and he's not cut, and I want so badly to touch him. I feel like I'm having an out-of-body experience with the amount of want coursing through me.

"Stop," I say through my orgasm-soft brain.

Parker groans from deep in his gut. "Please."

"Put a condom on your dick and get up here."

Parker hurries to sit on his haunches, then puts on a condom even quicker. He looks a little unsure as he climbs up the bed to settle on top of me, but I don't care. I wrap one arm around his shoulders to hold him close to me and reach the other down to take his cock in my hand. The surprise that flits across Parker's face makes me grin up at him, my smile doubling when Parker dips down to take my mouth with his own.

The kiss is messy and furious as I work his cock over, enjoying the hard feel of him in my hand. He feels so different from myself, but so familiar at the same time.

"Fuck, Mace," Parker says with a groan against my mouth. "I've wanted you so long."

"Fuck my hand, pretend you're fucking me. You're inside me, branding me so that everyone knows I'm yours. Can't you feel it?" I lift my legs to wrap them around his hips, working him over harder to emulate fucking. "You're making love to me, Parker."

Parker takes my mouth and lets out a groan that sounds borderline painful as his hips snap hard into me. The condom fills as he stills, his panting breaths passing into me to give me renewed life after so many years just *living* without really living.

"I love you so much," Parker whispers against my still kiss-wet lips.

"I love you too."

Parker drops his forehead to mine. "You're mine, all mine. Stay with me."

"I'm here," I promise, softly kissing the corner of his mouth. "Always."

Parker nods against my head, takes a steadying breath, then kisses me deeply once more. We kiss for so long that we grow hard again, and this time I switch the condom on Parker's dick and take him into my mouth. I'm nervous and fumbling, trying to find the ways that make Parker's hands tense on the bedspread, the pressure that makes Parker's hips lift ever so slightly with his inability to hold back. And when he finally comes with a pained groan, I can feel him grow against my tongue even through the condom, and it feels like everything is going to be okay with the world as long as we always have this, have each other. Because Parker's the first person to break through my defenses, to really *see* me without judgement or disappointment, and I'll never let him go.

CHAPTER 12
PARKER

"You guys could have *tried* to be quiet," Reid says, arms crossed and a glare aimed our way when we enter the living room.

I go to say something snotty back—the words are on the *tip* of my tongue—when Mason makes a frustrated noise that drags Reid's hard gaze to his brother. Mason levels Reid with an intense look that Reid shrinks a little under. I have to fight back the smile that threatens to break free at the sight.

"Reid, you need to get over your problem with Parker," Mason demands, voice steely.

Reid's eyes narrow. "Why? It's not like he's going to stick around if you're just fu—"

"Do not finish that sentence," Mason says, his gaze gone cold. "I'm in love with him, and Parker's here to stay. So get over your issues because I'm not dealing with infighting for the next forty years."

"Forty years?" Reid says in astonishment.

Mason shrugs as if he didn't just drop a nuclear bomb. "He's not going anywhere. I'm in love with him."

Reid just keeps staring. "It's not... It's not just physical?"

Dante groans at Reid's stupidity and looks toward us with clear pity in his eyes. I do feel a little bad that Reid can't read obvious cues. Mason's annoyed gaze turns on Reid but softens when he swings his gaze toward me and holds out his hand in a silent show of affection. I take his hand in mine, forgetting about Reid, forgetting about everything crumbling around us, and focus on the perfect feel of Mason's hand pressed against mine.

"It's so much more than physical that I can't even try to explain it," Mason admits softly, sky-blue eyes shimmering as he looks up at me.

I lean over to kiss him softly, ignoring the annoyed gasp that comes from Reid's direction. The front door barges open and lets in a blast of cold winter air. Soon the sound of Claude stomping his feet on the outside mat echoes around the entryway. When I pull away from Mason to turn around, I find Claude carefully taking off his boots on the mat before stepping farther inside.

"Did not take long," Claude says with a childlike grin. "I have found a buyer for Mason's government dirt."

Mason looks skeptical. "What's the price?"

"Jacob will go free."

"And they'll stop going after us," Mason supplies, eyebrows lifted in this sexy devil-may-care sort of way. I can't help but grin in delight at his newfound confidence. Although, I think Mason was always this way, it was just often buried under the anxiety, which he still feels, but maybe just a *little* less with me standing by his side.

Claude blinks slowly. "That is a big ask. Do you all not understand you are wanted dead?"

"No, we get it," Dante pipes up from the sofa. "But we don't care."

"It will go both ways," Claude argues.

"And then they'll have to tell us who they are so that we don't go after them," Reid points out.

Claude looks a little put out but slips his shoes back on and returns outside with an irritated huff. I let go of Mason's hand after giving it a good squeeze, then move to sit beside Dante on the couch. Tilting my head back against the soft cushions, I let my eyes drift closed for a moment. Everything is too much. It's all too much.

The sound of the sliding glass door has me opening my eyes to glance over at Hayden. His shoulders are still hunched, eyes a little lifeless, and I can't contain that feeling of utter asshole that I felt earlier once Mason pointed out that maybe what I said was insensitive. But it never crossed my mind that Hayden didn't know the plan, didn't know the entire point of why Jacob was so obsessed with him. Although, after Hayden's reaction, after Hayden called him Jake multiple times, I'm starting to wonder if maybe I don't know the entire point of why Jacob is obsessed with our insufferable boss.

Hayden plops down at the dining table with an air of resignation, like he can't give any more up before losing it all. I consider crossing the room to comfort him, but I fear saying or doing the wrong thing again and making everything worse. So, instead, I stay on the couch beside Dante and smile at Mason when he lowers himself beside me, pressed against my side in a way that settles all the jagged, aching pieces inside of me from Jacob's absence.

"Alexis is kind of cool," Reid says, effectively breaking the tense ice.

Dante snorts fondly. "Of course, you'd think so. She's fucking terrifying."

Reid smiles with stars in his eyes. "I want to be her when I grow up. Maybe I'll go to law school."

"A lawyer who moonlights as a vigilante," Dante says with a curl of his mouth. "Sexy, baby."

Reid practically preens. "Right?"

"You'd hate being a lawyer," Mason points out with a roll of his eyes. Everyone turns to look at him. "Reid, you'll get kicked out of court the first time you sass back at a judge when they do something you don't like."

"Well, I'd make them listen."

"Of course," Mason replies sarcastically.

"Anyway," Reid says, changing the topic. "What are you going to do now that you're not digging up dirt for Uncle Marc?"

Mason shrugs. "Don't know. I think I'll take some time off and help all of you get this drama settled, then I can figure myself out, see what I want to do."

Hayden shifts uncomfortably at the table, drawing everyone's attention toward him, but everyone else shifts their gazes away, while I can't seem to look anywhere else. I pat Mason's leg before standing and then heading into the kitchen. I go about the familiar routine of boiling water in Mason's kettle. I make two cups of peppermint tea and settle at the table opposite Hayden.

Hayden circles his uninjured hand around the warm mug, mouth twitching at the corners like he wants to say something.

"Is there anything you want to tell me?" I ask softly.

Hayden keeps his gaze on the tea. "No. We just need to get Jacob out."

"Alexis will handle it."

"Maybe." Hayden hums and sips the still scalding tea. His gaze shifts to mine, sharp and assessing. "Robin won't speak to me."

"I'm sure there's a reason."

His laughter is pained and bitter. "Yeah, maybe. Or maybe I've spent the last four years trying to do everything perfectly to earn favor, and it was all for waste. In so many fucking ways actually. I'm never good enough, ever. It's my fault Jacob is where he is and..." He curses and tosses himself back against the chair, closing his eyes tight so he doesn't have to look at me. "You look nothing like him, but you look identical at the same time. It's fucking cruel."

"Well, my hair is much longer."

"Yeah," Hayden says with a forced laugh. "Those same fucking eyes though."

I reach across the table to rest my hand on Hayden's. "Boss, it's okay to love him, to love us."

Hayden yanks his hand away as if he's been burned. He stands sharply and stares down at me like I've said the most disgusting thing he's ever heard. I feel a little lightheaded at his attention. I'm not used to it.

"Love is a useless emotion, Parker." Hayden's chest heaves as he stares down at me, pain radiating from every molecule of his body. "At least for me. Now stop trying to perform *woo woo* emotional crap on me, and let's figure this shit out."

I watch Hayden's back as he heads toward the front door, no doubt to go pester Claude into hurrying the deal up. But just as he's about to yank it open, Claude pushes in with another blast of freezing air. They stare at each other for a moment before Hayden lifts his chin in defiance under Claude's careful gaze.

"I have a deal," Claude announces, hands in his pockets as he rocks back on his heels. "Psycho redhead, you better have as much dirt as you insinuated."

Mason skewers Claude with a look so pissed off that Claude looks a little shaken by it, which pleases me more than I can ever say. Beneath all his anxiety and fears, Mason is a little spitfire, and I'm so excited to watch him flourish.

"Well, if you can hand over enough dirt to take down twenty percent of the District of Columbia, then you will be a very beloved man."

Mason stands from the couch in a hurry. "I have more than that after years of digging."

Claude hands Mason a piece of paper. "Here's an IP address to upload the data to, and in return Jacob will be let free without any charges, and you'll all be free to go about what you have been doing for years."

"But we need to know who we're dealing with so we don't go after them," Reid points out again.

Mason hurries off to the second-floor study before he can hear Claude's reply. But I'm a little thankful because I'm not sure Mason needs to know.

"Your buyer is"—Claude looks down at his phone with furrowed eyebrows—"Johnathan Wagner?"

Reid gasps. "As in... one of the Wagner brothers... the dudes who own literally everything in the United States?"

Claude shrugs. "I do not know them, but they are buying the data, and they are the ones who wanted an end to your behavior. But now that they have their data, they are not afraid of you."

"But why would these guys want us to stop?" Dante asks in confusion, looking around at all of us.

"They're the top conservative donors in the country," I tell him, thinking about the different ways in which this current news could fuck us forever. This feels a lot like getting into bed with the enemy. "They lobby Washington hard, and they basically shape the country. They are probably highly motivated in keeping the status quo, if not in favor of it being skewed toward the bad guys."

Hayden groans in frustration. "Are we signing anything or is this a handshake deal?"

Mason reappears from upstairs, a grin on his beautiful face. "It's uploading now."

Claude smiles. "Let me make a phone call."

"Do you stay on the payroll after this?" Hayden asks, eyes squinted in suspicion at Claude.

Claude shrugs, all easy and free. "I did not expect the good side to pay better than the bad. Look at me as Switzerland. But I have a feeling you are all going to need me even more now."

"Why?" Hayden levels a glare at Claude. "What do you know that we don't?"

"Well... I assume you will not be stopping what you have been doing, and I also assume you will be going after the Wagner family now, yes?"

Hayden's grin is cruel and cunning, sending a shiver down my spine. "Yes. You assume correctly, Carver."

The grins they exchange are terrifying in their cruelty. Claude disappears outside again, leaving us all a little anxious and waiting with bated breath. I wrap my arm around Mason's shoulders and tug him to me, needing the weight of his body against mine to steady the fraught nature of the moment. He tangles his fingers in the shirt at the small of my back as he glides his lips over the edge of my jaw. In that moment, I realize how far we've both come, but still how much farther we have left to go.

Claude returns for the third time, a wide grin on his face. "Well, boys, we are officially in business. When do we go after the Wagners? And not to spill the beans—that's the phrase, right? Regardless, there is a sector of boys like you in every large metropolitan city in the continental United States. Did you know?"

Everyone, including me, looks to Hayden in question. But Hayden just looks confused as hell, and also a little hurt.

"What?" Hayden whispers in disbelief.

"Yes. That is why I was sent to torture blond psycho, to see if we could infiltrate the spiderweb."

"It's just us," Hayden says, almost as if trying to reassure himself.

Claude shakes his head firmly. "No, children, there are hundreds of you. But we will tackle that at another time. Now, we must get the other one of you out of jail. I will tell that beautiful small attorney the deal."

Claude disappears again. Reid makes a disgusted noise, and I drag my attention to him. I thought maybe it was about me and Mason all cuddled up in front of him, but Reid's gaze is stuck on the front door.

"I don't trust him," Reid says with an attitude. "Plus, I don't forgive him for making my stomach a slab of hamburger."

"We're stuck with him for now." Dante wraps his fingers around Reid's neck and squeezes gently, making Reid go from tense and annoyed to relaxed. "He won't touch you again, I promise."

"He won't touch you either," I promise Mason.

Mason grins up at me. "I know. You give off the scariest touch-him-and-die energy. I'm safe when you're around."

Hayden makes a disgusted sound. "Surrounded by fucking couples. Fuck off."

Instead of Claude returning once more, Alexis throws the door open. She doesn't step inside, just puts her hand on her hip and stares us all down in obvious contempt.

"Well, let's go get Jacob," Alexis says with a small, delighted smile.

"Yeah?" Hayden jumps up from his seat in a flash. "Really?"

"Yeah, come on, crazy, let's go get him."

We all don't need to be told twice.

Alexis heads to her car, with no Claude in sight, and we all pile into my car to head to the local jail. Mason sits in the passenger seat, his usual spot now, and Dante and Hayden flank Reid, who sits in the middle. The ride is quiet and tense; all I can think about is Jacob. I feel like getting him out is the start of something I'm not sure we're all ready for at all. What is it going to be like between Jacob and Hayden now that Hayden knows the truth?

By the time we pull up in front of the jail, parking in a spot beside Alexis, Hayden looks like he's going to barf. The sky is cloudy, almost with the promise of snow, and it fits the mood that's hanging over us all. We all climb out of the car in silence and follow Alexis and her confident stride toward the jail.

She holds her hand up when we get close. "Stay out here. I'll go inside. He was fast-tracked, so he should be done with processing out any minute now. But the last thing I need is the five of you inside a jail where the cops can sniff your crimes out."

Dante leans down to sniff himself. "We smell like crimes?"

Alexis sneers. "Just stay out here."

"Dude," I say to Dante with a laugh.

"What? I'm curious... I don't want to smell like a criminal. I want to smell like expensive cologne that they keep behind the counter at Macy's."

"You smell like expensive cologne, buddy. It was a metaphor."

Dante blinks, then smiles. "Good."

Mason and Reid talk amongst themselves in whispers, while Hayden, Dante, and I stand around awkwardly waiting for Jacob to be released. The past almost day without Jacob was hell and just reaffirms to me that we have to finish what we've started so that we can all be free. I never want to worry about Jacob in jail again. I don't want to worry about him being somewhere that I can't protect him. After all, I was born with him beside me, and I don't want to go through a moment of life without him close enough for me to punch him.

After twenty minutes of tense waiting, the jail door opens to reveal Alexis grinning and a disheveled, tired-looking Jacob plodding along behind her. Hayden gasps beside me but doesn't move a muscle, but the rest of us do. Jacob is in my arms before I can even blink. His hug is tight, and I hug him tighter so that he knows it's real, that we're here and he's coming home.

"You smell like shit," I whisper into his ear.

Jacob's chuckle is laced with exhaustion. "I feel like shit too. The cops weren't exactly nice either."

I pull away to inspect him, noticing for the first time the black eye and cut lip. When I run my hands down his arms, he winces when I get to his wrists. They're bruised from the cuffs, and rage threatens to overtake me. But Mason appears at my back, calming me enough to keep my wits about me.

"You're coming home. Everything's okay now."

Jacob winces and glances at something over my shoulder. "Is it?"

I turn around to find Hayden looking anywhere but at Jacob, a fraught look on his face, blooms of red high up on his cheeks. Before any of us can say a thing, Hayden stomps back toward the car, and Reid chases after him.

Jacob turns back to me. "What happened to his arm? What the fuck, Parker? You couldn't keep him safe for twenty-four hours?"

I narrow my gaze at him. "First off, fuck you, and second, he punched a wall *twice* when he found out your entire role as fall guy."

All the color bleeds from Jacob's face. "What?"

"He didn't know! I thought he knew."

Jacob squeezes his eyes shut tight and goes silent. Dante slaps a hand on Jacob's shoulder, squeezing tightly in reassurance. "Come on, let's go home. You can get a shower and then we can figure everything else out."

Despite his personality dictating he argue, Jacob swallows his arguments and pride and lets us steer him back to the car. We all pile in, and in a strange turn of events, Hayden rides with Alexis back to the house. The car is even more tense and silent now, with Jacob staring forlornly out the window like he's in a sad music video. Mason and I just shrug at each other and make our way home. Hayden hops out of Alexis' car with a wave over his shoulder, disappearing into the house after keying the code that only I know in. Little shit.

When we walk inside, Jacob freezes at the sight of Claude

sitting at the kitchen table eating a Granny Smith apple. Unease prickles under my skin at the fact Claude is smart enough to get through alarm systems, into the house, and act like it means nothing at all if the apple and easy grin is anything to go by.

"What the fuck?" Jacob says the moment his eyes land on Claude.

Claude just grins cheerily around said apple. "Welcome back, brother. We are team now!"

Oh, fuck me.

CHAPTER 13

MASON

The house quiets once Claude leaves, everyone settling into their own corners. There seems to be an unspoken rule that shit's about to hit the fan, and everyone wants to spend the final evening minding their own wounds.

Once upon a time I would've hated my house being full of people, especially people who I don't know as well as Reid, but it oddly settles me in a way to have them all here. The small noises they make, the fact they all wash their hands when they come in and out, their shoes stacked by the front door. Sure, they could have an illness that drops me to my knees, but maybe life is made up of more moments than being afraid of a cold that incapacitates me. I think my therapist will be very proud of my recent developments.

Can't tell her my growth is from my recent escapade as a murderer though.

After a scalding hot shower to settle my nerves, I pace in front of the bed, waiting for Parker to join me. It's been thirty minutes since he disappeared into a guest room with Jacob and Hayden, Dante and Reid downstairs blowing off steam outside.

The door finally creaks open to reveal an exhausted-looking Parker. I smile at him, hoping to ease his nerves, and wouldn't you know, it works? His shoulders lower a little and his eyes get that glint in them that makes me feel like the only person on the planet.

"How is he? Did they talk?"

Parker shakes his head furiously. "Hayden refuses to speak to Jacob. Jacob spoke at Hayden for a few minutes, but then Hayden left to go to your study, and Jacob and I just caught up." Parker runs a hand through his hair. My eyes get caught on the movement, wanting again to touch him in a way to comfort him, the feeling still foreign but nice. "I feel like the team is falling apart when we need to be the most together. I don't know how to fix it."

I take a few careful steps closer, close enough so he can feel my warmth, but we aren't touching. "You're doing your best. It's not your responsibility... I don't want to misstep, but I think some of this is Robin's fault."

"I... I kind of think you're right." Parker reaches out slowly, and I let him take my hand. We sit down side by side at the edge of my bed. My heart beats wildly when he tilts his head to rest it on my shoulder. "I've spent all these years thinking I was so *cool*, trying to be the best that I can be, to earn approval, make us the best, but I'm starting to wonder for what. This whole plan... What's the purpose? We've never been told. Hayden has this blind belief that it's for the greater good. If we just keep going, we'll find out. But we all graduate this spring and still don't know anything. I don't know anymore, Mason. I can't let Jacob be the fall guy. And now

Robin's brought Claude into the ring... I don't understand anything anymore."

I turn my head and press a kiss to Parker's forehead. "Maybe we feel things out, play from the inside."

"What?"

"Well, when Claude kidnapped Reid, he wanted to know who else was working for Robin. There are more of you. More of us. Maybe we need to connect with them to figure this all out, and maybe we need to consider that Robin isn't as altruistic with their motives as you've been led to believe."

Parker lets out a pained sigh. "I can't entertain the thought we've been doing all of this for *bad* for the past three years. The entire point was for *good*."

"I know, but this is the first step. We can figure out the rest as we go. Right?"

Parker tilts his head to kiss my chin, making me shiver. "You're so smart."

Oh. I can tell where this is going. "Parker..."

"Distract me. I don't want to think about this anymore. I want to think about you for a little while."

"Me?"

Parker nods against my neck. "Always you."

He slips his hand under my shirt at the same time that I fall back on the bed, letting his bodyweight fall on top of me. The room is dark, sun set a while ago, but it's easy to see Parker even in the shrouded darkness of my room. He lights everything up, the darkness never that dark when I'm in a room with him. This love inside me could threaten to make me burst into a million little supernovas until maybe we become one.

"Hey," I whisper, trying to get his distracted attention.

Parker lifts his head from where he'd been kissing my throat, eyes dark and needy. "Yeah?"

I trace my fingers over his eyebrows, settling them in his hair to tug a little. "We'll figure all this out. I promise. But for now, I'll let you take me apart and put me back together, if that's what you need. It's okay for us to need each other, I think."

Parker smiles softly, tilting his head to nuzzle his cheek against my wrist. "You're so soft, but not when I give you a gun."

I snort with laughter. "That's my tagline. Soft, except when he has a gun."

"Not always soft," Parker murmurs lowly before crawling down my body to take me apart.

+

A gentle knock at the door wakes me up from a deep sleep. Parker is still sound asleep on his side of the bed. *His side.* My brain does a little happy dance at the idea of that before remembering someone at the door woke me. I maneuver myself out of the bed as best I can without disturbing Parker.

Hayden stands at the door, illuminated only by the night-light in the hallway. His breaths are coming heavy and his eyes are haunted.

"Hayden?"

Hayden lifts his hand to clutch at his chest. "I can't *breathe.*"

"Come here," I murmur, opening the door until Hayden gets the clue to walk through. Parker stays asleep despite the clumsy steps Hayden takes into the room. I scurry into the bathroom, rifling through my cabinets until I find one of my emergency antianxiety meds. Is this legal? No, but Hayden is hurting, and he won't help himself, and it looks like I'm the one who is going to end up ensuring all of these guys don't fall apart at the seams mentally.

Hayden collapses onto the floor of the bathroom beside me, eyelashes wet with tears, chest moving rapidly in the way I know intimately—his brain is telling him too many things at once.

I tip out two pills and fill a glass with water, then kneel beside him. "Take them."

Hayden does it without any further prompting. I sit beside him on the bathroom floor, only the darkness and the quiet between us, until Hayden's breathing slows and he tips his head back against the wall.

"I've failed them all," Hayden whispers brokenly.

"How so?"

Hayden shakes his head. "I've known for a while. Robin isn't *one* person, but many. I figured it out one day, you see, when the emails started to look different. One formats with a size smaller text, the other likes to use hyphens for no discriminate reason. I don't think Robin is bad, but I'm starting to think..." Hayden tilts his head to the side to pierce me with another haunted look. "I'm not sure what we're fighting for anymore. And Jacob... Jake..."

"Yeah," I urge him.

"I won't let anyone make Jake the fall guy. Anyone else but him."

"Why?"

Hayden snorts. "Oh, Mason, you're smarter than that. If you have to ask, you haven't been paying attention."

He's right, but I think he needs to say it, instead of me guessing. "Maybe you'll feel better saying it out loud."

"No," Hayden firmly denies, sounding more tired as the moment goes on. "Jacob can't love someone like me, no one can."

"Why?"

Hayden lets out a pained puff of air. "Nobody can love me. I killed my own brother."

The air grows thick with tension, then immediately falls as Hayden slumps in exhaustion against the wall, effectively knocked out. It's at that moment that a sleepy Parker pushes through the bathroom door, hand rubbing his slightly stubbled cheek.

"Oh," Parker says in shock.

"He had a panic attack," I tell him.

Parker wakes up immediately at my words. "Hayden did?"

"Let's get him into our bed."

Parker and I work together to get Hayden up, but maneuvering a large Greek god into the bed isn't easy, despite our own size. But we get him into the center of the bed, both of us lying down beside him, our hands tangled over Hayden's body.

"He told me something," I whisper into the room.

Parker closes his eyes. "Keep it between you two. He wouldn't want me to know. If he wanted me to know... I'd know already."

"I suppose you're right."

"I love you, Mason, but we need sleep. I think a war is coming. Don't you feel it?"

I squeeze Parker's hand but don't answer him, just waiting for him to fall asleep on the other side of his best friend. The air is electric, and the hair on my neck stands on end. I do feel it. In my bones. Something or someone is after us, and Claude is a stopgap until we can figure out where to go from here.

But it's not just the four of them anymore—they've got Reid and me as well. I've ached to have a family for so many years, never feeling enough for Reid, or even for myself, and I can't help but find it a little ironic that I found family among these murderers filled with honor. After all, I'm one of them now too. If one of them goes down, we all do. That's the rule now.

My brain is quiet and happy as I fall asleep with Parker's hand in mine, seeking out that one more touch that'll do the trick. Quiet and lovely, that's what Parker's love is to me. And then we sleep.

EPILOGUE
MASON

One Week Later

Time has never moved so slow, even counting that first week after my parents died. Each day that goes by, the boys pull further apart, distanced in some way that feels like it's my fault, but it's not. *Just the anxiety*, I remind myself as I thoroughly clean the kitchen for the fourth time this week. At least Parker doesn't say anything, doesn't give me odd looks, he just accepts my need to clean as part of my *what the fuck do I do with all these anxious thoughts in my brain* process.

"I'm going to grab the last of my stuff today," Parker says from where he leans against the kitchen doorway.

"Oh?" I ask, rubbing my chin against my shoulder.

Parker smiles sweetly. "I want to live here, and the boys will get used to it."

"Maybe," I murmur grumpily, unsure if Jacob will ever forgive me.

"Jacob will get over it," Parker says as if reading my mind.

I narrow my eyes. "Are you sure?"

Parker just tucks his hands into his dress pants, showing off those epic forearms of his that I'll always be obsessed with. He catches me staring at said forearms and his smile grows a little more teasing, and even a little sexy. He likes when I ogle him, even if nothing is going to come from it. And I like ogling Parker, I like looking at him, thinking about all the things we can do one day if my brain lets me. But it's also nice to know that it's not a requirement to ever do anything if I don't want to because he loves me as I am.

Parker loves me. How odd.

I toss the wet sponge into the sink and turn around, leaning my back against the cold granite. Parker stays where he is, patient as always, waiting to see what I'm willing to give today. And the anxiety is high enough that I'm not willing to give anything except to look and maybe be ogled in return.

"You know," Parker says with a teasing lilt to his voice, "maybe we should have our own signals, like what you and Reid have."

There goes my heart.

"Yeah?" I ask, voice breaking on the word.

Parker grins like a schoolboy with his first crush. "Yeah." Parker tilts his head, studying me like he always does. He lifts his hand and taps just over his heart. "This means I wish I could hold you." Parker trails his fingers over his chest to tap them against his throat, where his blood pounds away. "This means I'm thinking about doing very dirty, dirty things to you." He slowly trails his fingers up to his lips, pressing a kiss to his finger. "And this means I want to kiss you so badly it hurts."

Don't cry, I tell myself. Fucking romantic asshole.

"Which one do you feel right now?"

Parker's grin turns shy. "All three?"

"Oh fuck you!" I shout through laughter.

And that makes Parker's grin turn even broader as he tucks his hands back into his pants. "Want to come with me to grab my stuff? Maybe you can see Reid?"

"I can't clean anymore, so... sure. Why not?"

"That's the spirit."

Parker tugs on his jacket that hangs beside mine at the front door. I stare at my hoodie for a moment, the one I stole from Parker and never returned, the one that smells like him and me combined. Parker tilts his head at me as I continue to stare.

"Will you put my hoodie on for me?"

Parker's eyebrows furrow. "Put it on you?"

"Yeah."

"Can I touch you or...?"

I nod instead of answering with words, watching quietly as Parker gently takes the hoodie down from the hook and steps closer to me without touching. I lift my arms up and hold back a grin when Parker delicately tugs the sleeves down my arms, then grin like a lunatic when my head pops through the neck of the hoodie. A flush blooms across Parker's high cheekbones as he stares at me, some emotion that I can't parse now, but I hope maybe one day I'll be able to.

"You're adorable," Parker says gruffly.

"It's your hoodie," I point out.

Parker sighs. "Yeah, that makes it even more adorable. Maybe tonight we can watch *The Goonies* again. I kind of like it now, you know. Those kids are a bit like all of us."

I snort as I follow Parker out to the garage. "Amazing. Maybe we should watch some other movies of that decade. I think you'd *really* like *The Breakfast Club*."

"Why?" Parker asks as he uses his epic forearms to reach out to turn on the car.

"No reason." He will *love* Judd Nelson's character. Pretty easy to call.

"If you say so, Mace."

"I like that nickname because it's cute, but also, isn't that a pepper spray? I'm cute but also violent if I need to kill someone."

"Very true," Parker says amicably.

"You're very agreeable today."

"I'm preparing for Jacob's wrath in ten minutes."

"He won't be mad at you," I reassure Parker with a defeated sigh. "He'll be mad at *me*."

"It's impossible to be mad at you."

"Tell that to Reid," I murmur under my breath.

The ride to the boys' house is quiet except for the soft tones of the grunge music Parker prefers. I've never been much of a music guy, but his music is really starting to work for me. Mostly because it kind of reminds me of Parker, and I love *anything* that reminds me of him. Sometimes when he's gone to class or visiting Jacob, I'll put on a playlist of the songs I've gathered over the past weeks and just think about Parker. What a lovely thing.

"Don't let Jacob get to you," Parker reminds me as we head into the house.

I hum absently and veer away from where Parker heads up the stairs, and instead head toward the perpetually warm living room, where it's easy to spot Reid curled up in the chair by the fire. His sketchbook is in his hand like always, but he looks more tired than usual, his hair a little flatter.

"Still stressed out?" I ask while taking a seat on the sofa beside him.

Reid hums and scratches at the paper with his pinkie. "Would be easier if we were all under one roof."

"Sorry, Reid, but it's Parker's decision."

"I know," Reid replies, which is a step in the right direction. No arguing means Reid's not actually upset, perhaps he's just sulking. "You're here to grab the last of Parker's stuff? Probably easier to live apart now that Robin has been MIA since Jacob got out of the slammer."

"The slammer," I guffaw.

Reid tosses a grin at me over his shoulder. "I'm the levity they need."

"That you are." I lean forward to peek at his sketchbook, but Reid hides it from me with a glare. "Just curious."

"It's not finished. Anyway, you know I never share my drawings."

"You do with Dante."

Reid blushes and stares down at his open sketchbook like I've caught him committing some sort of cardinal sin. I wasn't trying to be an asshole, I was just trying to point out that maybe Reid shares himself with Dante because he feels safe in a way he doesn't with anyone else. It might upset other people, but it would never upset me. I'm more myself with Parker than I am with anyone else, and sometimes that's the way the cards are dealt.

Parker interrupts us as he comes down the stairs with a duffel bag tossed over his shoulder. Jacob follows behind him, a miserable, resigned look on his handsome face. I want to say something to make it better. To... I don't know... apologize, but I bite my tongue because this is Parker's battle, not mine.

"Hi, Mason," Jacob says from behind Parker, shoulders hunched.

"Hi." I shoot Parker a concerned look, then smile softly at Jacob. "We can do weekly dinners at my house. That way you get a break from cooking."

Jacob only looks slightly mollified. "That sounds nice."

"Oh my god, you're all acting like Parker is dying," Reid cries from his chair, slamming his sketchbook shut. "We should all be more worried about Hayden and his refusal to leave his bedroom."

Jacob returns to looking distraught at the mention of Hayden.

"He won't leave his bedroom?" Parker asks in confusion, because for a very perceptive guy, he's also wildly oblivious.

Reid rolls his eyes and groans, skewering me with a *you deal with that* sort of look. I just shrug and smile, because Parker is a lot of things, but he's not oblivious when it comes to me. Shoving up from the couch, I pause in front of Reid to tap my nose. Reid sighs and taps his own nose, although he seems personally aggrieved by the entire situation. Where is Dante?

As if summoned by my thoughts, Dante wanders in from the kitchen with his hand buried in a bag of chips. Jacob rolls his eyes when Dante holds the bag out for him. With a shrug, Dante brings the bag back to his chest and surveys the room.

"Lots of tension," Dante observes.

Parker sighs loudly. "I'm grabbing the last of my stuff."

Dante winces. "Oh snap. Can I turn your room into my shoe closet?"

"Dante!" Reid screams.

Dante winces again and continues eating his chips. "I'll let the dust settle, bro, sorry. We're all a little antsy because there's no missions. You don't even have solos?"

Parker shakes his head. "Not even a peep."

"Damn." Dante whistles and shoves more chips into his mouth. "We are kind of screwed," he says around a mouthful.

"Well, on that note, I am going back home." Parker turns and slaps Jacob on the bicep. "I'll text you tonight. Make sure you leave food at Hayden's door, I guess. Waffles always work."

"He left the plate outside his door all night last night," Jacob says glumly.

Dante shrugs when I look to him for an answer. Parker just sighs and heads back toward the front door, not even bothering with a response to Jacob. I give everyone a wave and follow Parker out the door, hoping not to add to his stress. The five-minute drive back to the house is silent. Parker didn't even turn the radio on. My anxiety ramps up a little bit, worried that maybe Parker will change his mind about me, about us, but I try to keep myself in the moment because I can't control the future.

Burying my hands in the hoodie pockets, I follow Parker into the house, not knowing what to say to make this moment easier or better. Everything is so fucked right now. I don't know how to help any of them, nor do I know how to help Hayden after his perilous confession to me in the bathroom just last week.

"I'm not upset with you," Parker says succinctly the moment he drops his duffel bag. "I don't want your brain to think things that aren't true. I'm tired and frustrated and I wish Jacob would let me cut the umbilical cord."

"Oh."

Parker smiles tiredly. "I knew you were thinking the worst."

I wince. "Sorry."

"Don't say sorry." Parker takes a step closer so that I can

feel his warmth, smell his delicious aftershave. The anxiety from earlier has softened, and now all I can think about is Parker in front of me, needing comfort, needing *me*, and suddenly my decision to push myself is a lot easier. "Mason, I—"

I step forward and wrap my arms around his neck, putting our faces just a few inches from each other. Parker holds his breath, arms hanging loosely at his sides.

"Put your arms around me, hands on the small of my back," I tell him softly.

Parker immediately does as I said, his hands warm and firm through the hoodie. The touch makes me move a little closer, closing that inch of space between us so that we're pressed together toe to chest. I can feel his hummingbird heartbeat through his shirt and my hoodie, can smell the soft, warm smell of him, feel the loose hairs from his bun curling over my fingers at the nape of his neck.

"I love you," I whisper between us.

Parker takes a quiet breath. "I love you too."

"Everything's going to be okay as long as we have this, right?"

"Right," Parker agrees like the good boy he is. "You're doing better."

"I'm pushing myself."

Parker closes his eyes tight. "Thank you."

I curl my fingers in the hair at his neck, rubbing gently, petting him like a dog like he often says. The tension bleeds from his shoulders, making me smile.

"You're my happily ever after," I whisper, just before pressing a soft kiss to his mouth. His lips open ever so slightly, and I can feel the soft exhalation he lets out against my lips upon hearing my words. Touching Parker so often feels like a dream—like a sort of prayer I'm lifting up to the god of kind touch. And all that anxiety melts away as my brain shuts off under the soft slide of his mouth against mine, the feel of his hands against my back, and the knowledge that even though everything else in the world might go to utter shit, in Parker's arms I'll always be the safest.

I go to pull away, but Parker murmurs, "One more touch," against my mouth, and I can't deny him when he asks so sweetly, even if my heart stings a little at the quietly uttered plea. All the touches in time. As long as we have this, have each other, nothing else will ever matter.

The End

(for now)

Hayden and Jacob are next (early next year but no pre-order yet). Want early news on the dramatic finale of the One for All trilogy? Sign up for my newsletter now.

ACKNOWLEDGMENTS

First and foremost, I must thank the team that makes every book possible. JJ, Hannah, and Lexi. Y'all listen to me whine about giving up, tell me to knock it off, and give me the courage to keep going. None of these books would ever see the light of day without you.

JJ, thank you for giving me the safe space to let Mason bloom to life. Sometimes he was so personal that I felt like I didn't know him, but you gave me the gentle nudge to keep pursuing the greatness that is loving a character that is sometimes hard to understand.

Hannah, when I felt a little lost with Mason you said "give him a gun". You are worth your weight in gold, rubies, and puppy kisses.

Lexi, thank you for *always* having my back. Reid is always for you.

Abigail, thank you for the sensitivity read, grammar errors and all. Your childhood cancer insight was beyond valuable.

Marie, for all the *I don't know if I can do this anymore's* and your poignant *you can do this because you have before.*

Last but not least. I must thank my kid, who sees my nose taps, and taps their nose right back. Parenting is hard most days, but a blessing every day. I love you to the milky way and back, kiddo. All of this is for you.

ABOUT THE AUTHOR

Maya spends most of her time imagining happily ever afters for the characters that live in her head. If she's not plotting how to heal broken hearts for her characters, then she's spending time with her precocious daughter. She loves baking competitions, listening to the same song on repeat for months, and discussing the latest pop culture event in a group chat with her best friends.

ALSO BY MAYA JEAN

Sweet Southern

(escorts finding love against a southern backdrop)

The Husband Experience

The Former Fake Boyfriend

The Remarkable Lover

The Long Refrain

One for All

(college vigilantes and suspense)

Call It Desire

One More Touch